A Penknife in My Heart

by NICHOLAS BLAKE

"A dramatic . . . book."
— Francis Iles, *Manchester Guardian*

"Storytelling of exceptional competence."
—James Sandoe, *New York Herald Tribune Book Review*

"Style brilliant, happenings realistic, tone somber and suspenseful."
—L. G. Offord, *San Francisco Chronicle*

**Titles by Nicholas Blake available
in Perennial Library**

NICHOLAS BLAKE

A Penknife in My Heart

PERENNIAL LIBRARY
Harper & Row, Publishers
New York, Cambridge, Hagerstown
Philadelphia, San Francisco
London, Mexico City, São Paulo, Sydney

A hardcover edition of this book was originally published by Harper & Row, Publishers.

First PERENNIAL LIBRARY edition published 1980.

ISBN: 0-06-080521-8

80 81 82 83 84 10 9 8 7 6 5 4 3 2 1

For
Barbara and Geoffrey

Author's Note

After a British edition of this book had gone to press, I discovered that the basis of its plot is similar to that of a novel by Patricia Highsmith, *Strangers on a Train,* published in 1950 by Harper & Brothers and later made into a film. I had never read this novel, or seen the film, nor do I remember ever hearing about them. My own treatment of the basic idea—the switching of victims—is very different from Miss Highsmith's. But two of the chief characters in my story, I found to my consternation, bore the same Christian names as two in hers: these have been changed; and I should like to thank Miss Highsmith for being so charmingly sympathetic over the predicament in which the long arm of coincidence put me.

Contents

When my back began to smart
 'Twas like a penknife in my heart.
When my heart began to bleed
 'Twas death and death and death indeed.

Nursery Rhyme

A Penknife in My Heart

1 *The Nelson Arms*

IT WAS shortly after entering the bar of the Nelson Arms on a Saturday in August, 1955, that Stuart Hammer first perceived how he might commit the perfect murder.

He had come into the estuary an hour before nightfall, on the last of the flood, and anchored *Avocet* by the stern so that she would swing round and point seaward when the ebb started to run, for he had no wish to spend the night in a river that, at low tide, would be little more than a deep ditch between the saltings. Indeed, but for shortage of beer he would not have ventured into this tricky channel—one he had never sailed before. But the map showed a village half a mile upstream, and where there was a village there would presumably be a pub.

Stuart Hammer lowered himself, with an empty crate, into *Avocet*'s dinghy. There had been no sign of human life or habitation since he had ghosted into the river mouth on his auxiliary engine. The expiring light showed, even here, nothing but water, dunes and ashen-colored grass. "Godforsaken bloody spot," he muttered as he pulled away, the current pushing him toward Brackham Staithe. A sharp bend in the channel swept *Avocet* from his sight. Glancing over his left shoulder, he saw lights a couple of hundred yards away; the stream broadened into a pool where a ghostly flock of dinghies lay moored. Stuart threaded his way through them, and made fast to the hard on the northern bank of the river.

"Brackham Staithe," he grumbled. "The yachtsman's Mecca. They can have it. Handy place for smuggling, though, it could be."

Sailing single-handed—and he did it from choice, not necessity—had got Stuart Hammer into the habit of talking to himself. At any time, though, he preferred his own conversation to that of almost anyone else—a fact of which his numerous acquaintances and boon companions were blissfully unaware.

Brackham Staithe was very far from being a yachtsman's Mecca. Apart from occasional visitors, those who sailed here were all local residents; so the place was dead enough except at weekends, when the salt-water lagoons, with their roughly marked and awkwardly placed sandbanks, made an interesting obstacle race for dinghy enthusiasts.

Tonight being Saturday, the Nelson Arms was crowded with them, slaking the demoniac thirst induced by salt-water sailing, and giving off the forced animation that is generated by a group of people who have little interest in one another outside the hobby which has brought them together. Men in jerseys, shorts or stained trousers; weather-beaten women who looked as if they were made of rope rather than human flesh; one or two of those impossibly exotic girls who are to be found on the fringe of every sailing community, and seem, with their linen suits and painted nails, to have strayed in from the pages of *Vogue*.

In this gathering, Stuart Hammer's arrival went almost unnoticed. The locals assumed him to be a visitor staying at the Nelson Arms; the few visitors took him for a local. A copper-haired girl of extreme beauty, sitting very close to a man on a settle opposite the door, glanced up at the short, broad-shouldered figure who entered, vaguely noting the piratical look of his beard, his reddish-brown face and the shade he wore over one eye.

Pushing his way to the bar, Stuart ordered a pint of mild and bitter, and two dozen of bottled beer to replenish his crate. He ran an eye over the room as he drank. Deal and pitchpine; hard chairs and settles; trade advertisements; beer-slopped tables. It was poky and smoky, dead-alive—just the place for these inland mariners, he thought. With some red leather and chromium he could do wonders for it: a few converted ship's lanterns instead of these blinding naked bulbs; keep those prints on the wall over there—frigates and ships of the line in action—customers like a bit of ye quainte olde.

An oleograph above the bar, representing the sailor after whom the pub was named, caught Stuart's attention.

"The patron keeping an eye on things, eh?"

"I beg your pardon, sir?" said the innkeeper.

Stuart jerked his head at the picture. "Nelson."

"That's right, sir. He was born in these parts. Over to Burnham Thorpe, see? Your first visit, sir?"

"Yes. What? Oh, yes. I'm—"

Stuart's voice faded out. Above the oleograph ran a long mirror, set at an angle so that it reflected the far side of the room. What had attracted Stuart's eye was the red

head sitting so close to the dead-beat chap on that settle;
what held it was the chap himself. He had never seen a
chap so obviously at the extreme end of his tether. There
was no mistaking it: Stuart Hammer's experience in
Coastal Forces and later in the Palestine Police had
taught him the signals you made when you were about
to rush round the bend. The couple were talking in
undertones—a conversation which, one felt, had been
going on, going round in circles, for hours; perhaps for
weeks and months. Leaning on the bar, his bright blue
eye turned dreamily toward the couple, Stuart followed
this conversation. It was, of course, quite inaudible in the
shindy: but one of his curious and cryptic skills was that
of lip reading.

He had acquired it as a boy, in hospital, during a long
period of deafness which followed a fracture of the base
of the skull. He had kept it up, as a man, for the secret
feeling of power it gave him. Stuart Hammer loved
power, and was never quite satisfied even by the large
measure of it which his forceful personality provided for
him. Since becoming personnel manager in his uncle's
Midland factory five years ago, he had had ample opportunity among the clattering machines to exercise this gift.
It was part of the boyish streak in him and went with the
glee of feeling incognito, of growing a beard and continuing to wear a now quite unnecessary eyeshade during
his holidays at sea. Because it was perfectly genuine, this
boyish streak was all the more disarming, and therefore
all the more dangerous.

Stuart Hammer watched the lips moving. He all but
heard the rasp of utter emotional exhaustion as the white-
faced chap spoke:

"... But, darling, we've been into this over and over

again. I *know* Helena. She'd never consent to divorce me. She enjoys her cat-and-mouse game far too much. There's nothing she'd like better than to know I want to get away from her and to play me on the line."

"Poor Ned! So she has you hooked?"

"I suppose so. In a way. When you've lived with some-one for ten years—"

"Well then, there's nothing for it but—"

"No! Laura, I won't give you up. I'm only alive when I'm with you. Everything else is unreal. Do you *want* me to give you up?"

"Oh, *please,* Ned! You know how I love you. But it'll go bad in me—I can't go on much longer with this hole-and-corner life. It's so squalid and messy."

The man looked up, his haunted eyes meeting Stuart Hammer's for an instant. After a pause, the girl's lips moved again.

"I still don't see why you can't just leave her, my darling. At least it'd bring things to a head. Even if she refused a divorce or a separation then, you'd at least—"

"Oh, we've had this out a dozen times."

"It's not as if you and she had any children."

"It's not as if I had any regular income, either. You keep forgetting that. If I left her, she'd bloody well make sure that *I* supported *her* for a change. What would you and I live on?"

"When your play's put on, darling—"

"When the cows come home!" A gloomy, savage look showed on the man's face. His mouth twitched uncon-trollably and he jerked back the lock of dark hair that lay over his wrinkled forehead. His eyes glared sightlessly at Stuart Hammer across the room. "I wish she was dead," he said.

"Oh, Ned, you mustn't!"

"And so do you, my beautiful love, and so do you."
The two gazed deeply at each other for a moment. The
reckless look that accompanied his last words took years
off the man's face and gave it extraordinary charm. The
girl gripped his hand, pressing her thigh close to his; a
complex expression came and went on her face—triumph, perturbation, tenderness were in it. She was one
of those very rare women to whom some subtle blending
of innocence and experience gives a special quality of
elusiveness. Not that this thought occurred to Stuart
Hammer, who was as insensitive as he was shrewd.
"What she wants," he said to himself, "is less natter and
more bed. And I don't see that bloke giving it to her."

He turned to the innkeeper. "Many people staying
here?"

"Yes, sir, we're full this weekend."

"Don't I know that red-headed girl over there? An
actress. Now, what's her name?"

"That'll be Mrs. Saunders, with her husband. Came
last night. They're staying till Monday. So she'd be an
actress, would she? Fancy that! Such a quiet, nice-spoken
couple." Breathing heavily, the man craned his neck to
see over the heads of his customers.

"Well, I thought I'd seen her in a play somewhere,"
Stuart vaguely replied. Glancing at the couple again, he
read the white-faced man's lips saying:

"I wouldn't lift a finger to keep her alive. She's a
hopeless case. If she was an animal, somebody'd have put
her out of her misery long ago." He was trembling all
over.

"I want you, Ned," the girl whispered. "Let's forget
her for tonight."

"You go up then, love. I must have a breath of air—it's foul in here. I shan't be long."

Stuart Hammer's eye roved round the bar. No one here he knew. No one who knew him. With a curt good night to the landlord, he picked up his crate and went out of the room a little ahead of "Mr. Saunders."

"Excuse me," he was saying a moment later, "could you give me a hand with this crate to my dinghy? Strained my arm a bit yesterday."

"Of course," replied Ned. "Lovely night."

The masts of the sailing dinghies stood motionless in the air; the ebb lisped and chuckled along their sides as they strained at the moorings, all facing one way like a flock of sheep, pointing upstream. The hard was deserted. In the light of a quarter moon the mudbanks of the channel were smooth and molded, like chocolate blancmange. The two men stowed the crate in the dinghy.

"Stretch my legs for a few minutes," said Stuart Hammer. "My boat's a few hundred yards downstream. You a sailing man?"

"I've done some dinghy sailing. No deep-sea stuff. Hoping to borrow a boat tomorrow."

"Smoke? Oh, my name's Hammer, Stuart Hammer."

"Thanks." Ned did not vouchsafe his name. He took some deep breaths, inhaling the delicious night smells of water, mud, dune, grass, tar, then lit Hammer's cigarette and his own. A light went on in an upstairs room of the Nelson Arms. Laura would be getting undressed now. Ned smiled in the darkness—he would stay out a bit longer, to sharpen anticipation. The stranger was strolling away from the hard and the pub, Ned at his side, along the riverside path, their feet silent on the grass, till fifty yards farther on they came to a ramshackle seat.

"Staying long?" asked Hammer when they had sat down.

"I really don't know. My wife has to get back to London on Monday morning. I might take a few days more. I'm a free lance just now."

"Lucky chap." Stuart's personality, like some exotic weed, seemed to flower extravagantly there in the darkness. "I say," he went on, with a rush of boyish impulsiveness, but keeping his voice low, "if you *are* at a loose end for a few days, would you like to join me in *Avocet*?"

"Well—"

"Sounds like a crazy suggestion from a total stranger. But the fact is my partner got ill—had to put him ashore last Wednesday. Normally *Avocet*'s easy to sail singlehanded; but now I've strained an arm—"

"I don't know if I'd be much help," Ned dubiously answered. But the idea attracted him. It would at least postpone his return to Helena.

"Don't you worry about that. If you can sail a dinghy, you'll pick it up quickly enough." Stuart Hammer fell silent a moment, pondering how best to approach the crucial point. This chap is obviously a bit of an egghead, he thought: therefore the bluff, breezy manner is indicated: appeal to his romantic side—these sedentary blokes all dream of being men of action.

"Ever tried your hand at smuggling?" he suddenly asked.

"*Smuggling?* Well—no."

"Any moral scruples about it?"

"I—I haven't really thought. Depends what, I suppose."

"How do you mean?" The glow of his cigarette lit up Stuart Hammer's keen blue eyes, fastened upon Ned.

"Well, I'd draw the line at drugs. That's a filthy game."

"Quite. But watches, brandy—that sort of thing?"

"Oh, I'd pass them. I'm a bit of an anarchist."

The stillness of the night, the faint moonshine, the presence of this compulsive stranger combined with Ned's own abnormal state of mind to cast a singular unreality over the encounter. Muffled sounds from the pub, a dog barking in a farm beyond the village, seemed like noises out of a dream.

"I'll put my cards on the table," said Stuart quietly. "I'm fetching a consignment from the Dutch coast on Wednesday. Must have some help with the sailing part of it. You'd get a cut, of course—wouldn't be less than fifty quid, might be more. Bit of excitement for you, too. Story in it, maybe—you're a writer? But no real danger: I've got the thing taped. Are you on?"

Hammer's voice and manner were so infectious, so agreeably challenging, that his companion perversely felt the need to put up at least a token resistance.

"But why me? I mean, you don't know the first thing about me. I might trot off tomorrow to the nearest Revenue and Excise boys."

Hammer chuckled. "I've knocked about. I can pick out the odds and sods. You're all right."

Ned felt an absurd glow of gratification. "O.K., I'll come in," he said.

"Good man. By the way, what *is* your name?"

"Edwin Stowe—Saunders. Ned for short."

"Double name? Stowe-Saunders?"

There was no use trying to hide the slip. "I'm Saunders down here," Ned replied, flushing a little.

"I get you. 'Nuff said." Stuart Hammer at once became extremely businesslike. He told Ned exactly where and when he would pick him up on Monday night, and how Ned should get there. He gave him an alternative rendezvous for a couple of hours later, in case either of them should miss the first one. He advised him to bring nothing but razor, toothbrush and sneakers; there were spare jerseys, oilskins and sea boots on the *Avocet*.

"And one thing more. It's to safeguard you as much as myself. No one must know you're joining me. Repeat, *no one:* which includes—er—Mrs. Saunders. *Compris?*"

"Of course."

"It's not of course, old man." There was an edge of steel beneath Hammer's affable, brusque tone. "You've got to cover your tracks when you leave this place. Whatever story you think up—off for a few days to potter round the Norfolk churches—whatever it is, it must account for your temporary disappearance and give no lead to our little expedition. You've never met me, never heard of me—savvy?"

"Yes."

"You can always change your mind. If you don't turn up at either rendezvous, I'll know you've had second thoughts. People do."

"I'll be there," answered Ned, slightly nettled.

Stuart glanced at his wrist watch. "I must get out of this ditch before it dries up. No, not together. Give me three minutes' start. Be seeing you, Ned."

The stocky figure disappeared into the darkness. A few minutes later, as he sauntered back to the Nelson Arms, Ned heard the faint splash of a dinghy's oars passing him

downstream. He realized, with a start, that for the last
quarter of an hour he had only once thought of Laura,
and that was when the stranger had mentioned "Mrs.
Saunders."

"I'm still here," said Laura.

"Yes, love. Sorry."

"You mustn't brood. It's a lovely day, Ned, and we've
got it all to spend. Don't think about her, my darling."

"Yes." But it was not Helena that Ned had been
brooding about. The extraordinary encounter last night
—he could not put it out of his mind: he had not dreamed
it, yet it had the vivid unreality of a dream that, on
waking, seems both absurd and bodingly prophetic.

Ned sifted the powdery sand of the dune through his
fingers. Smuggling? If I were a smuggler, is it conceivable that I should pick out a total stranger in a pub, tell
him my name and the name of my boat (well, of course,
they may have been false names), and invite him to join
me? A crazy risk. Or was it? Stuart Hammer could just
deny everything, if I rang up the police now. It'd be my
word against his. But how could he be sure that I'd not
have the authorities alerted, ready to catch him with the
contraband on his return? Do I look like a desperado?

Ned found he had murmured the last words aloud.

"You do, sometimes," said the girl. "Why?"

"Oh, nothing."

"A sort of contained excitement," she went on dreamily, "like a pot simmering with the lid on. I noticed it last
night."

"Not so contained, was I?"

"I don't mean *that.*" Laura turned her bowed head a
little away; the fine coppery hair veiled one cheek. There

was nothing coquettish in the motion—she often bent
her head and looked away when she was pursuing some
thought. Yet this elusive movement always worked upon
Ned Stowe like a charm—the most flagrant, abandoned
look could not provoke him half so much.

"I don't mean that," she was saying. "Last night, when
you came upstairs, you looked like a small boy gloating
over a secret—no, that's not quite it—a small boy who's
accepted a dare, and isn't letting on: a bit frightened;
seething with excitement."

Ned was never nearer telling her the whole story. He
loved it that Laura should be able to read his mind thus:
it was another sign that they were meant for each other.
Helena, of course, had the same flashes of intuition; but
they were the lurid flashes of the neurotic, showing him
up in the worst possible light.

"You bet I was excited," he said. "Or don't you know
yet how you get me worked up?"

It was the first time he had prevaricated with Laura,
deliberately misled her. The personality of Stuart Hammer must have impressed itself on him very strongly.
Well, he had given the chap a promise. And anyway,
there was a certain gratification in keeping a secret from
Laura—his first secret—for a few days: he would tell her
all about it when they met in London the following week.

"What are you thinking about?" asked Laura.

"Doesn't the village look pretty? I'm trying to photograph it on my mind. . . . All the places we've been
together in. They ought to put up a plaque in each of
them."

" 'Here Ned Stowe and Laura Camberson were
happy.' "

"Happy?" He sighed, and the lines on his face deepened. "If we weren't always seeing everything for the last time, my love—"

"When I'm with you, I see everything for the first time."

From the dune where they sat, the row of waterside houses, half a mile away, resembled a ship rather than a village. The walls, painted black or tarred; the window frames, picked out in white, like gunports; the upperworks of wooden balconies: a long hull of houses, riding low above the water, looking from here as if it and not the land was their natural element. The river and the lagoons were dotted with sails under the huge East Anglian sky. A brisk wind blew from the east, but the two lovers were sheltered by the dune. Ned had got the loan of a sailing dinghy for the morning. After an adventurous hour dodging about in the channels, with a good deal of centerboard work by Laura—for they frequently ran onto the edge of underwater sandbanks—they had landed on this islet, which lay between the main lagoon and the sea.

"Why do we have to go back?" said Laura. "Let's build a house on this island."

It did not irritate Ned. They knew each other well enough to accept such fantasies for what they were worth.

"We'll come back again, won't we?" he said.

"Will we?" She was gazing up at him, but there was something withdrawn in her gaze. "Will we?" she said again, in a hurried mutter, averting her eyes now.

He took it as a plea for reassurance. He had no inkling that she had just, not decided, but known with dreadful conviction, that they must part forever.

"Of course we will, love. Why not?"

"Kiss."

As he took Laura in his arms, she began shaking all over and sobbing distractedly.

Ned did his best to comfort her, but he felt momentarily detached, almost cold toward her. Perhaps ten years of Helena has used up my stock of pity, he thought.

"I'm sorry," said Laura at last. "All this is killing me." Her uncontrolled gesture took in the furtive assignations at out-of-the-way restaurants, the guarded telephone calls, the elaborate planning for brief meetings, the false faces they had to wear when in public together, the lies and the everlasting shiftiness upon which their relationship had rested ever since that day, four months ago, in the television studio.

"It's not doing me much good either."

A flight of terns, flashing in the sunlight, swift and frantic as a volley of guided missiles out of control, did their aerobatics over the little beach where the dinghy was drawn up. Gloomily, Ned watched them. He knew that his nerves were almost frayed through; yet it was only by holding himself in, by incessant watchfulness over word and movement, that he could prevent himself splintering into mad, centrifugal fragments.

"I won't let you go," he muttered, answering a question in his own mind.

Laura was lying on her back, her hair tumbled over the pale sand, eyes closed. He looked down at the blue veins of her eyelids, the high cheekbones, the long, naked arms like white snakes, the big body that was so fluent and delicate. She should have children, he thought—my children. He studied her attentively, like a map; the map of a country which, though he had been there often, would remain endlessly mysterious to him.

He had known her long enough to feel that he could never break away from her without mutilating himself beyond recovery.

"What'll you do when I'm gone?" she said. The words came like the distant echo of an explosion in his own mind. His voice shook uncontrollably.

"You're not going to leave me, Laura?"

"I mean, tomorrow, and—"

"Oh, some sailing. Pottering about."

"What'll you do for ballast without me?"

"A few hundredweights of sand."

"Hundredweights! You are a beast!" Laura was sensitive about her large body. She never quite liked even Ned's making a joke about it; and these moments of self-distrust, self-depreciation, in a woman who appeared to others so calm and invulnerable, always stirred in her lover a deep tenderness.

"It's the most beautiful body in the world," he said, laying his hand on her.

"No, my darling." Laura sat up. She held his hand in her lap, looking down at it; then she let go of it, and moved a little away from him. "I can't say what I have to say when you're touching me."

Ned's face tightened. He seemed to be bracing himself for a too-long-expected blow.

"Ned, I should have said this ages ago, but I've kept putting it off," Laura went on, in a low, hurrying, breathless voice. "I *cannot* go on much longer with this sort of life. Oh, darling, don't look like a stone image—please try to understand how I feel. I know it sounds selfish, but I must have *something* to build my life on."

"Isn't my love—?"

"I'm a woman. It's not enough to know that you love

me. I can't live in the moment—I've got to have some sort of stability. I know it's just as bad for you—worse probably, with Helena on your mind too. I've seen you getting more and more on edge. It'll drive you into a nervous breakdown. Oh, Ned, I'm afraid of damaging you any more."

"But why now? Why do you have to choose our happiest moment to—?"

"Just because it was the happiest. When we were sailing the boat together just now—we understood each other so perfectly, without saying anything. Don't you see? We ought to do everything together, all the time, or give each other up. This isn't just a love affair, for either of us. Half a loaf is worse than no bread. We can't live on snatched hours; some can, but we can't."

"You mean I must go back to Helena? Haven't you any idea what you're condemning me to when—?"

"Don't be angry with me, my darling, *please*. I would live with you openly, as your mistress, if she won't divorce you. But I must live with you. I can't stand being treated any longer like a—like a dirty post card."

"Laura!"

"Put yourself in my place. Wouldn't you feel just the same?"

"Perhaps. But I'd choose to have you, *on any terms*, rather than to part," he answered with quiet force.

After a pause, she said, "That's because you're a man. It's different for you. But I hate dragging on, never knowing—"

A sea gull wailed overhead. Ned rose abruptly. "Put on your jersey, sweetheart. We'd better go. The tide is ebbing."

2　*The Water Test*

NED STOWE drove Laura into Fakenham to catch a late-afternoon train. There seemed no point in her staying another night in her present state of mind; and, though he knew she half wanted to be coaxed or forced out of it, a perverse impulse stopped him doing so. They drove past the heavy cornfields, through the villages dripping with roses. Ned remembered nothing of the drive afterward except the feel of her hand in his: a pall of fatality hung over them, as if they were taking each other to the slaughter. On the platform, Laura said, "I shall always be there"; and a little later, "Don't hate me." They might have been ghosts, engaged in the last minutes of some posthumous and futile reunion. As the train moved out, Laura gazed back at him, leaning through the window, never taking her eyes from his, her own face all hollows and shadows, set in the expressionless beauty of a death mask. What message was she trying to send him? A waft of courage? A plea for understanding? He did not know. At one point she just raised her hand—a tentative, timid movement which stabbed him with remorse. He was glad, afterward, that he had waved back.

Returned to the Nelson Arms, he stood for a while in their empty bedroom, staring at nothing, like a victim of concussion. Then he forced himself to write a short letter to his wife—he'd had some jolly sailing, the pub was comfortable, he was off tomorrow for a sight-seeing trip, didn't know where he'd land up but a letter poste restante Yarwich would find him on Thursday; he hoped all was well at home—the letter of a prep-school boy to his mum, he thought bitterly.

It was only after sealing it up that he realized it gave Helena his present address; if she suspected anything, an inquiry agent would soon discover that he had stayed here with another woman. Well, let her discover, if she wants to. Let's have a showdown. It was the nearest he could come to it. He knew, and despised himself for it, that he had not the moral fiber to make the first move and tell his wife about Laura.

In an attempt to take his mind off his present misery, Ned began planning how he should follow Stuart Hammer's instructions. He was staying at the Nelson Arms incognito—unless anyone here had recognized him from the occasional photograph that appeared in the *Radio Times* and the *TV Times*, there was no danger of "E. Saunders" being identified as Edwin Stowe. He would spend tomorrow pottering about the Norfolk villages in his car, moving steadily south so as to arrive in Yarwich after nightfall; leave the car at a garage, with his luggage locked in the trunk—he could take what he needed for the voyage in his mackintosh pockets. Stuart Hammer had told him exactly how to get from the town center to the derelict slipway in the outer basin which was their rendezvous. There must be no mistake about this: a man inquiring the way to such a spot, late at night, might rouse unwelcome curiosity. He would buy a large-scale map of Yarwich tomorrow, and memorize the route. It was important, also, to arrive at the rendezvous at the exact time, for he did not want to be noticed hanging about near the deserted slipway. If all went well, he would virtually disappear from view as soon as he left the Nelson Arms in the morning; there would be nothing to connect "E. Saunders," let alone Ned Stowe, with Stuart Hammer and the *Avocet.*

The only danger point seemed to be the slipway. If he arrived there too soon, or the mysterious Hammer was late, and some local accosted him on the lonely fore-shore, he must have a convincing story to account for his presence there. As a writer of television plays and adaptations, Ned had seldom found any difficulty in churning out plausible fictions; but now his mind was a blank.

Going downstairs, he had a drink with the landlord, and several with himself, before supper. Laura's departure had left him stunned, without feeling, but now his heart began to ache intolerably. His whole bloodstream seemed to be poisoned, with self-pity and with a corro-sive resentment—against Laura, against his wife, against his own weakness—which the drink only stimulated.

"Pity the missus couldn't stay the extra night," said the landlord.

"What? Oh, yes." Ned came to himself with a start. He was about to add that she had had a message recalling her to London, when he realized it would be a stupid lie —they had received no letters or telegrams here. "Yes, she's got to start work early tomorrow."

"Keep actresses busy, do they, sir?"

"Actresses?"

"I understood Mrs. Saunders was on the stage."

"Oh, no. She's a studio manager."

This clearly meant nothing to the landlord. "Gentleman who came in last night said he'd seen her in a play."

"He's mistaken." Ned's face began to twitch, and he turned it away.

"Thought he recognized her, anyway. Gentleman with the eyeshade. A stranger here."

Stuart Hammer recognize Laura? He gets more mystifying all the time. More likely he just wanted to get off with her, thought Ned. Perhaps his invitation to me was the first move in a campaign. The jealousy always smoldering in him flared up. Laura Camberson at twenty-seven, thirteen years younger than himself, had a reputation for easy-come, easy-go. A certain passivity lying deep beneath her vivacious manner—a sort of sexual fatalism, as Ned judged it—had made her unable to resist the men who swarmed to her. The first time they had met, at a party after a television play, their eyes encountered across the length of the studio and held one another in a long, exploring gaze, till Laura rose, walked like an automaton through the group of people she'd been talking with, and came over to sit beside him. Presently he took her home to her flat, where they fell onto the bed with each other as if poleaxed.

"I really don't make a habit of this sort of thing," he said afterward.

"I'm glad," she replied. She did not say, then or later, that she didn't make a habit of it either. Remembering it now, Ned thought, "She may be a bitch, but she's always been an honest bitch."

He believed she had been faithful to him since then: he believed her when she told him she had never loved anyone as she loved him. But her truthfulness, her fidelity hardly mattered any more, for she had got herself into his system like a virus and he felt that, whatever she did now, he would never be rid of her.

Perhaps Laura's threat to leave him was made so that he should be forced to decide between her and Helena. Perhaps, on the other hand, when Stuart Hammer came into the pub last night and saw Laura, a long look was exchanged—the same questioning, answering look as Ned and Laura had exchanged at the party four months ago. Why else should Hammer have suddenly chummed up with him? Why else should Laura suddenly decide to go? The thoughts writhed and lashed like snakes in Ned's brain.

At 10:30 the next night Ned walked out of the garage where he had left his car and, with the sensation of moving into a dream within a dream, directed his steps toward the rendezvous. The market square of Yarwich, with its elegant eighteenth-century town hall floodlit; timbered almshouses; a main street of rather garish shops; a cinema, a church, a river bridge—he registered these as landmarks on the way. Like most provincial towns, Yarwich went early to bed. Once he had left its center and was walking through the streets of smaller houses which stretched toward the docks, Ned hardly met a soul. He paused occasionally under a lamp to check the name of a street with a list taken from his mackintosh pocket: in the hotel, where he had dinner, he had worked out his route with the help of a large-scale town map.

A quarter of an hour's walking brought him to the

inner basin. Wharves, a fish market, Customs & Excise
buildings, derricks, a collier tied up near a gasworks. The
night felt colder here. There was a compound smell of
gas, fish, seaweed and oil. The water lay stiff and gleam-
ing like black treacle against the wharves.

Ned turned left and, crossing a set of railway lines,
moved along the waterfront. He was ahead of time, having allowed himself half an hour in case he should lose
his way; but everything had been so easy—inevitable as
progress in a dream. He knew exactly what would come
next: a row of warehouses, a footbridge over an inlet of
the river, a chapel for seamen, a public garden, a yacht
club, a—

"Evening."

A torch was flashed briefly in his face. Ned suppressed
a violent impulse to run for it. A policeman emerged
from the shadows between two buildings.

"Lost your way, sir?"

"No, thanks. Just taking a walk. I'm not trespassing or
anything, am I?"

Ned was impressed by the careless coolness of his own
voice. So, apparently, was the policeman.

"That's all right, sir. Good night."

"Good night."

He sauntered on, his heart still pounding. Odd that he
should have felt so guilty. He wasn't even a smuggler.
Yet.

Past the yacht club. A jetty, curving its stone arm pro-
tectively round a cluster of small yachts and dinghies. A
rusting M.L., stripped to a hulk, canted beside the sea
wall. A hundred yards further, the slipway. Five to
eleven. The moon was behind clouds, and the wind blew
colder. Ned moved into shelter behind a ramshackle

wooden boathouse, then peered out over the dark water. A few masthead lights. Silence, but for the steady burring of the wind. Shivering in his thin mackintosh, he felt for his cigarette case. No, better not: might as well play this game thoroughly, childish though it is.

Distant church clocks began striking eleven. When they ceased, the silence flowed back. Did I dream the Stuart Hammer episode? thought Ned; then, with a sickening lurch of the heart—or am I getting delusions? am I going mad—going mad? A nervous breakdown, Laura said. Is this it?

A lisp of water: oars creaking in rowlocks. The darkness by the slipway shaped itself into a boat and a man. Ned came out from the shelter of the hut, stepped cautiously along the slipway.

"Good man," said Stuart Hammer. "In you get. Take an oar, like a good chap; I'm lying quite a way out."

It was odd, sitting on a thwart beside this total stranger, who smelled of whisky and pulled with short, economical strokes, giving an occasional glance over his shoulder to check their course. Ned felt a curious shyness and an equally inexplicable desire to win the man's approval.

"Had no trouble?" Hammer grunted presently.

"No. Apart from running into a policeman on the dockside."

"You did, did you?"

"I just said I was going for a stroll. He wasn't in the least suspicious."

"Did he see your face?"

"He shone a torch on me for a moment."

"That's not so hot."

"Well, you never suggested my wearing a false beard," Ned replied, rather nettled.

"And nobody knows you're here? You've not been dropping sly hints to that popsy of yours?"

"Certainly not. Now look—"

"O.K., O.K. Good enough. Harder on your oar—the tide's pulling us off course."

Stuart Hammer was very much in command. When they reached the *Avocet,* he sent Ned up the side first, telling him to put on some jerseys and sea boots he'd find in the locker above the starboard bunk in the cabin. Ned jumped to it, hardly giving himself time to look round the cabin, which seemed very luxurious with its red leather, polished teak and electric light. When he emerged, he helped his companion to haul the dinghy aboard and lash it on the cabin roof. In a few minutes they had the jib broken out, the mainsail up and the anchor weighed, and *Avocet* was leaning over for the long beat toward the open sea.

"Your arm seems better now," Ned remarked.

"Yes, thanks. I've been taking it easy. Tighten your jib sheet, old son; we might make it on this tack. She sails very close."

"Seems a lovely boat. Bermudan sloop—is that right? I've never sailed in anything bigger than a dinghy."

"Yes. Had her built for me last year on the Solent. She's handy enough. But you can't go too far afield in a six-ton sloop. I could do with something bigger."

"Do you race her?"

"No. That's a mug's game. Can't stick the racing types —clannish lot, you know. I prefer plowing my lonely furrow. Anyway, I'm too busy."

"What's your job?"

"Personnel manager in my uncle's factory. Beverley's.

At Norringham. Godforsaken place, but it's a living. Of sorts."

Ned began to look around. The shore lights were receding. The lighthouse away on their port bow flung its sweeping beam, from a low headland, over the neck of water which led to open sea. The masthead of *Avocet* shifted gently, with the vessel's movement, against the whey of cloud far above. The great mainsail curved up into the darkness, like a sculptured abstract. A buoy whipped past and went wallowing backward, as if they were at anchor and it was racing shoreward. Ned felt a mounting exhilaration: his troubles were falling behind him, in *Avocet*'s wake; he seemed to have cut himself adrift from all responsibility. He stole a glance at his companion's face, in profile to him, lit up momentarily as the lighthouse beam scythed round on the water just ahead.

"Go below for a bit, chum," said Stuart Hammer, jerking his head toward the invisible lighthouse. "Coastguard station there. Don't want them to spot I've a crew with me."

Ned did as he was told, moving in what felt like the compulsion of a dream. This is part of Hammer's plan that he and I should not be seen together, he thought: cautious chap, for all his piratical appearance; wants to protect me in case there should be any trouble later, after I've left the ship.

He moved to turn on the electric light, which he had switched off previously before coming on deck, then desisted. If Hammer wanted to give the impression he was sailing single-handed, it'd be bad to have the cabin lit up. Ned groped his way to the portside bunk and sat down. Every ten seconds, as the lighthouse beam struck through the portholes, the cabin sprang out of invisibility, then went black again. For some reason, this alternation of pitch darkness and blinding light set up a growing uneasiness in Ned's mind. He found himself counting the seconds of darkness till the beam should come round again, and shrinking from it as though it were a naked blade.

Presently a more strenuous movement of the boat, a harder thumping of waves on the bow and a louder rustle of water past the side told him they were out from the shelter of the headland into open sea. At Stuart's call, he returned to the cockpit, feeling the wind's full force now —north-northeast, he judged—and seeing a flash of spray lift itself like a phantom over the port bow to hiss against the jib and vanish.

"Want to turn in yet?"

"No, thanks. I'm enjoying this," Ned answered. "When does the operation take place?"

"The operation?" In the dim light of the binnacle lamp, Stuart Hammer's face had an odd expression, distrait but faintly mischievous. "Oh, yes. Tomorrow night. We'll be lying up on the other side tomorrow. Dutch coast."

"Diamonds?"

"Slacken your sheet." Stuart put up the helm, and they turned a little to starboard, till the wind was full abeam. "You like to sail her for a bit now? Get the feel of it? I'll make some coffee." Stuart gave Ned their course, then ducked into the cabin, calling over his shoulder, "Give me a hail if we start sinking."

Peering from time to time at the compass needle, Ned sailed *Avocet* on into the darkness. He was overanxious and tense at first; but the vessel looked after herself in this steady wind, needing little of the watchfulness, the constant changing of course, to which dinghy sailing had accustomed him, and he was soon able to relax.

Presently Stuart Hammer emerged, carrying two steaming mugs, with a bottle tucked under his arm.

"You like coffee with your brandy?" He poured generous measures from the bottle into a mug and handed it to Ned. "All right, I'll take over now. We'll be crossing the coastal shipping lane in half an hour or so."

Ned could see already the navigation lights of ships in the distance.

"Must be a boring business tooling up and down the coast."

"Oh, they prefer it. See more of their families. It's like a village street—the coastal shipping lane. I sailed from Wandsworth to South Shields once, before the war, in a gas collier: flatirons, they called them. The skipper knew every vessel we passed, like a neighbor—knew her captain was suffering from a duodenal, and her first mate kept pigeons at home, and her chief engineer was having trouble with his wife, and the steward's first cousin was a supporter of Newcastle United. Regular hive of gossip —the east-coast route."

Stuart Hammer, grown suddenly expansive, talked on. Ned found him a fascinating companion now; the brandy, warming his blood, gave Ned a feeling of security and irresponsibility, so that he did not notice at first, when Stuart fell silent, the measuring looks which he kept casting over his left shoulder or the unusual tension in his attitude at the helm. Finally, however, Ned screwed his head round. The lights of what seemed to be a large vessel were visible ahead, on the weather beam, not more than half a mile away, on a converging course. Ned regarded them with interest, hardly aware that Stuart was slackening the main sheet and turning a little more to starboard.

"Big chap," he said.

"Cargo liner. Scandinavian probably. Hope he's keeping a lookout."

A few minutes later it was borne in on Ned that *Avocet's* change of course would bring them pretty close to the ship out there, whose bulk was now becoming visible against the darkness. He felt exhilaration and an absolute confidence in his companion's seamanship.

"Going to ram her?" he said with a grin.

"Steam gives way to sail. Rule of the road."

"If she can see our sail."

A roar from the ship's steam whistle, sounding to Ned more like a threat than a warning, announced that *Avocet* had at any rate been spotted. Stuart Hammer answered it with a loud raspberry and continued on his course. He was eyeing Ned very attentively, but the latter, concentrated upon the rapidly narrowing space of water between the two vessels, did not notice this. Unless one of them gave way, *Avocet* was going to sail right across the stranger's bows. He could not make out whether the steamer was turning away: a succession of hysterical bellows—the sound of a giant howling in a nightmare—came from her steam whistle. Ned could see the snarl of foam at her forefoot, barely two hundred yards away now; she would slice *Avocet* in half if they met. How quickly could a steamer that size change course? A garbled memory came to him of some naval court-martial, at which it was stated that two battleships on converging courses had been bound to collide, whatever action the coxswains took, once they were within half a mile of each other. And that Hardy poem—"The Convergence of the Twain."

Ned glanced at Stuart Hammer. The man was staring at him; his teeth gleamed through the rakish beard. Ned suddenly knew that he was sailing with a madman who was determined to kill them both. The whole plan of this voyage from the start had been paranoiac—the secrecy, the queer rendezvous, the inevitable smuggling fantasy. A wave of panic broke over him, followed at once by an amazing backwash. All right, he's going to drown us, *and I don't care;* nobody will care—not Helena, not Laura— so why should I? This will solve all the problems.

He grinned back at Stuart Hammer. "Hope you can swim. I'm good for about thirty strokes."

"He's not changing course," said Hammer, in a curiously urgent voice, as if he was trying to elicit some response from Ned.

"So it appears."

"Nor am I. It's going to be a near thing."

"Obstinate chap, aren't you?" said Ned, amazed by the fatalistic calm of his own mind.

Avocet, which had seemed big as a house when they were alone with her in the night, was dwindling now to a toy boat as the cargo liner loomed closer, blocking out the sky. Fifty yards, forty, thirty—panic returned, coming up in Ned's throat like bile, but he fought it down. The two vessels were drawing together almost at right angles: it felt as though the sloop was being dragged, like a pin to a magnet, on to the steamer's great cutting stem.

At the last possible instant, Stuart put his helm down hard and *Avocet* swerved round to port. But the steamer was so close now that she blanketed the sloop from the wind. Rapidly losing steerage way, *Avocet* wallowed ever closer to the steamer's clifflike sides: instead of running right across the steamer's bows, she was in danger of colliding broadside-on. There were shouts, the ringing of a telegraph bell, the pounding of engines, a white face looking down from the rail. The steamer drove past like an express, ten yards away—hawsehole, lighted portholes, thrashing screws—and left *Avocet* tossing in the wake so violently that it seemed her mast must topple. Waves pounced onto the deck from queer angles.

Suddenly a searchlight beam reached out from the steamer's afterbridge and felt for them; and in the same instant Stuart Hammer seized Ned by the back of the neck and flung him down sprawling into the well of the cockpit.

"Lie still," he shouted. "They mustn't see you."

Avocet lay bathed in the searchlight's beam; then, her sails filling, she paid off onto her course. Ned was past amazement. This was the climax of the dream which had begun hours ago. He lay still, thinking nothing except that he was still alive.

"O.K., you can get up now," said Stuart when the steamer's searchlight had been switched off. "Sorry about that, but it was necessary. Didn't hurt you, I hope."

"No. Just surprised me."

"Good man. I see you've got your nerve with you all right."

For the second time since they had met, a word of praise from Hammer gave Ned quite inordinate pleasure. "Nerve? You scared the pants off me," he said. His mind felt light and clairvoyant. An extraordinary notion came to him. "I say, the object of the recent exercise wasn't by any chance to test my alleged nerve?"

Stuart Hammer smiled in his beard. "If I answer that, will you answer me one? Would I be right in saying that you weren't frightened just now because you didn't care a damn one way or the other?"

"I see you'd be a success as a personnel manager," replied Ned after a brief pause.

"Give me some more brandy. And help yourself." Stuart Hammer's voice deepened, becoming almost hypnotic for Ned. "What's the trouble? Domestic?"

The resonant voice; the strange personality—enigmatic, yet giving an impression of being absolutely dependable; the light-headedness of relief which Ned felt after their narrow escape; the unreality of his present situation, sailing into the blue with a total stranger on an illegal venture: all this prompted him to tell Stuart Hammer his story. Ned, in any case, was the type who finds himself imparting confidences to strangers much more easily than to friends. But this particular story he had never told fully to anyone. The need for absolute secrecy had meant that he could never talk about Laura, while some inhibition of taste or conscience had always prevented him from exposing even to Laura the whole truth about his married life—to reveal what a destructive influence Helena had been.

Avocet sailed on, riding the waves like a seabird, and Ned talked on through the small hours. What did it matter? He would never meet Stuart Hammer again: they lived in different worlds. To pour out the accumulated misery and rancor of years gave him intense relief, as though a tumor on the brain had been removed.

It was surprising to find his companion, whom he had judged to be a tough if eccentric extrovert, so interested and sympathetic.

"So there it is," Ned concluded: "a nice tangle of neuroticism, self-pity and futility. Afraid I must have bored you to tears." His voice shook uncontrollably. "And I don't know how I can stand it any longer."

"I see. Let me recap the situation." Stuart Hammer was brisk, purposeful. "You cannot live without this Laura of yours. *She* threatens to leave you unless you break with your wife. Your wife would never consent to a divorce, and you cannot afford to live apart from her since she has the spondulicks." He glanced keenly at Ned. "Moreover, you're frightened of her. She's vindictive—capable of anything. Ye-es, you're certainly up the pole, old son." Stuart paused again. "In war, it's destroy or be destroyed. And it can be the same in love. Not that I'd know about that personally—I'm not one of the Grand-Passion brigade."

"I'm being destroyed all right," said Ned bitterly.

"Well, somebody's got to go, and I hope it isn't you. From what you've told me, your wife would be no loss to the world—or to herself. Pity that sort of person can't be put out of their misery."

The words sounded to Ned like an echo. "I agree," he said, "but—"

"Well, you'd better turn in now, Ned. Have a good sleep. You need it."

"But what about—? I mean, don't we have to make plans for this smuggling affair tomorrow? I'm completely in the dark."

"Oh, that lark. Yes, well, time enough. I've been

thinking, though, we might go into business together."

"Business? What business? I don't—"

"For instance—" Stuart Hammer's voice came out of the gloom like a spell—"for instance, we might make a contract for disposing of each other's rubbish."

3   *The Unholy Pact*

AT 11:30 the next morning, Stuart Hammer, passing through the cabin to the galley, observed that Ned Stowe was still asleep. He stopped for a while and eyed him speculatively, as if trying to gauge the man behind the pale, lined, exhausted mask, which heavy sleep had not smoothed out or tranquilized. Stuart did not know so much about the highbrow type; but in his rolling-stone life he had come across all sorts, and he didn't doubt that he could manage this one, given time. But time was the one article in short supply for Stuart. Little more than a month remained before his uncle, Herbert Beverley, would come into possession of certain facts—facts which would be the ruin of Stuart Hammer's prospects: at the age of thirty-eight Stuart viewed with no favor at all the idea of having to start again from scratch. As he thought of his uncle—the one man he had never been able to swamp with his powerful personality—Stuart's face hardened and an inhuman look came into his blue eyes. Time. The seed he had so deftly planted in this fellow Stowe's mind last night might take time to germinate—more time than he could afford. Somehow, it must be forced. Well, Stowe had slept on it; now he had better be compelled to do a bit of ruminating. Stuart placed his strong, hairy hand on Ned's shoulder and unceremoniously shook him awake.

"Rise and shine, old man! You've been sleeping like a log."

"I'm sorry. I was dreaming that—What's the time?"

"Nearly midday. Lav and wash basin through there, as you know. I'll run you up some coffee and biscuits."

Ned yawned. The haunted look was returning to his face. "Are we there?"

"We're there." Stuart Hammer forbore to tell him that, after sending him to his bunk last night and making sure he was asleep, he had turned *Avocet* round. She was lying at anchor now in an Essex creek.

"I've got to row ashore," he said. "Be away for an hour or so. Make yourself at home. I'll be back to cook us a meal."

"Can't I do anything?"

"No, thanks. Just sit tight. Oh, one thing, old son—" Stuart gestured toward the portholes, across which the white linen curtains were drawn—"don't look out. There are some inquisitive folk hereabouts. Might be rowing over to take a dekko, y'know. We don't want them to see a face at the window."

" 'The white face of damnation.' "

Stuart brushed it aside, like a bull a cobweb. "I'm supposed to be sailing this boat single-handed. You and I have never met. Top secret." He grinned, making it all appear a jolly, boyish escapade. "I shall lock the cabin door when I go: just in case any kids get the notion of clambering aboard. You don't suffer from claustrophobia, I hope."

"Only at cocktail parties."

"Which reminds me. Plenty of booze in that cupboard. Help yourself if you feel like it."

When Stuart returned with the coffee he noticed Ned eyeing him in a furtive, incredulous way. The seed was starting to germinate. Now let him stew for a bit. . . .

They had a late and ample lunch, deliciously cooked by Stuart when he got back. Before and during the meal, he plied Ned with drink, talking about his own job in the Norringham factory. After they had washed up, Stuart said he was going to have a snooze.

"I was wondering if you ever slept."

"Oh, I sleep when I need it, all right."

"Lucy chap."

And Stuart Hammer did in fact go to sleep, placidly as a child, having set the alarm clock in his brain for 6 P.M. For three hours Ned sat on the opposite bunk, glancing now and then at the recumbent figure of his companion as if to assure himself that it had not vanished into the thin air of a reality against which the spruce little cabin seemed hermetically sealed, but most of the time fingering in his mind the extraordinary remark Stuart had made to him last night. While Stuart was ashore this morning, Ned had begun to explore it. It could not possibly mean what he thought it meant: but in the context, what else could it mean? Like a tarantula in a glass case, it horrified yet fascinated him. He could not prevent his mind's eye from reverting to it. He was safe from it, yet he wanted to let it out and see what followed. Gradually, though the grotesque loathsomeness of the idea remained, he was becoming acclimatized to its presence. Not once did he give a thought to the ostensible purpose of this trip: the smuggling venture was already back in the past, swallowed up by last night's events.

A gull cried—sharp, convulsive, rapid sounds, mounting, then dying away as the bird was swept to leeward over the sloop. With intense vividness, and a pain like that of extreme hunger, Ned remembered his last night with Laura. Her body had never been so sensual, so versatile. She was like a sea, rocking beneath him, drawing him deeper, curving above him; but at the end of it all, like the sea, she remained mysterious and unpossessed, withdrawing from him into her secret self. And so it always would be, he thought; and that is why no other woman will ever take her place.

Stuart Hammer came wide awake at five minutes to six, swinging his legs onto the floor almost as soon as his eyes opened. "Well, opening time, or near enough. Whisky, I think."

He filled their tumblers and raised his to Ned. "Cheers. Have you given my project your attention?"

"Your project?"

"Yes. I propositioned you, as we tycoons say, that we should go into business together, you remember."

"But—well, I mean, you surely weren't serious?" Ned laughed nervously.

"Never more so, old man."

"About the—the disposal of each other's rubbish?"

"I see we understand one another. Yes. Why not? Mutual advantage, y'know—and for God's sake don't look at me as if I was a maniac carrying a bomb."

Ned swallowed. "Well, it *is* an absolute bombshell for me. Why, damn it, here you are—unless I'm off my rocker—coolly suggesting that we—"

"Let's keep calm and review the situation. Uncle Stu will tell you a little bedtime story. Once upon a time there were two characters—M and N, we'll call them—who made life hell for all and sundry, but especially for two other characters, A and B. A would like to dispose of M: B has a similar yearning in respect of N. But for obvious reasons, neither A nor B feels like putting the job in hand. But wait, children! Suppose that A and B—"

"For Christ's sake!" Ned broke out, beginning to tremble all over his body. "If you must talk about this, don't wrap it up in—"

"Righty-ho. You want to get rid of your wife. I want to get rid of my uncle. I'm suggesting that we should do each other's disposals." Stuart Hammer's tone was as jovial now as when he had been telling his bedtime story.

"You obviously *are* crazy," Ned muttered, not looking at his companion.

"Do you really believe that? I wonder. Look here, old son. Tell me the honest truth—have you never thought of killing your wife?"

"Oh, sometimes I've come damn near to strangling her. But not in cold blood, not—"

"Never mind about the temperature. And what stopped you?"

"Well, damn it all, surely that's obvious. I just don't happen to be a thug."

"I'll tell you why you don't kill her. You're afraid of being hanged. That's why I haven't knocked off my uncle. In spite of all this sentimental cock talked by the people who want to abolish capital punishment, it's fear of being hanged that stops—"

"Oh, so you're in favor of capital punishment?" Ned tried to smile, but his face had gone stiff as a board.

Stuart Hammer did not understand irony. For the first time, he sounded impatient. "Stick to the point. What have you against my proposal? Moral scruples? But we've agreed the world would be better off—"

"For *God's* sake! Can't you realize how utterly fantastic this all is? You come along, a total stranger—"

"Oh, hell, I quite forgot, we've never been introduced. Of course the whole thing is off. But seriously, old chap, don't you see—the fact that we *are* total strangers is the nub of it all. Neither of us would have any motive, any connection with his victim whatsoever. Look at it this way. I dispose of—what's her name?—Helena for you. You arrange to be a hundred miles away when it's happening, so you've got a perfect alibi. Unless I bungle it, which I wouldn't, I'm absolutely safe too; I've never met Helena: I haven't any conceivable reason for—"

"All right, you needn't labor the point. I see the exquisite beauty of it all. I say," Ned went on suspiciously, "was this what you had in mind right from the start, when we met at the Nelson Arms? But how on earth could you have known that I—"

"Second sight, old man, second sight. Well, I don't mind admitting the smuggling plan was a pretext to get you on board." Stuart tossed the remains of his whisky down his throat. "I'm a great planner, y'know. In fact, when I found you had the right stuff in you, I turned *Avocet* round. We're back in home waters."

Ned hardly heard this. His mind was full of bewilderment and fear, all adrift. He tried to get a grip on himself. "Well, you picked the wrong man, then," he said, a shade too resolutely.

"Ah well," replied the other, after a pause. "That's

that, I suppose. No harm done. We go our separate ways. And Helena drives you into the nuthouse. Though I must say, if I had a girl like Laura to look forward to, I'd not let anything or anyone stand in my path. I thought she meant more to you than just an expendable pair of tits and what-have-you. You disappoint me." Stuart spoke with a flick of contempt.

There was a short silence in the cabin, darkening now with the twilight outside. *Avocet* stirred, rocking gently in the wash of a passing craft. Stuart Hammer refilled their glasses.

"Apart from anything else," Ned muttered, "how could you expect me to kill a total stranger in cold blood? I mean, for all I know, your uncle may be a thoroughly good sort of chap."

Stuart Hammer's eye flashed and went out like an Aldis lamp at the hint of weakening in Ned's voice. "Herbert Beverley a good chap!" he exclaimed. "If that's what's worrying you—look here, I'll run us up some grub, and then I'll tell you about my uncle." Stuart's experience of negotiating with shop stewards had taught him how to gauge the right moment for applying pressure or for relaxing it. When a chap's just beginning to soften up—when *in his own mind,* no matter how strong his external resistance, he has made an admission and given ground a little—then is the time to break off for a while and let the rot spread: if you pounce on the weak spot right away, your opponent rallies all his forces to cover it.

Grilling chops in the galley, Stuart Hammer thought out his next moves. First, he must present Herbert Beverley in the worst possible light, so as to weaken Ned's moral scruples. This fellow Stowe is an intellectual, therefore probably a sentimental Leftist, a humanitarian, and all that sort of cock: so I must make Uncle Herbert a domestic tyrant, a bad employer and a totally unscrupulous businessman. Secondly, reasoned Stuart with considerable shrewdness, Stowe is a writer of sorts, and writers must be particularly susceptible to words: if I discuss with him detailed plans for the two operations, on a hypothetical basis—this is how we'd do it if we were going to do it, but of course we aren't really going to, it's just as if we were collaborating over a play—then the fact of putting it into words will make it more real for him, more conceivable, more practical. And thirdly, there's the problem of guarantees. I shall have to kick off: so I must have a hostage, to ensure that he reciprocates when it's his turn. That's a knotty one. The usual blackmail devices wouldn't work, for obvious reasons.

Stuart needed more time to think. He left the chops to keep warm on the stove, and set about preparing a treacle sponge. Presently he snapped his fingers. Yes, that's his Achilles' heel all right. And a singularly unpleasant smile dawned on Stuart Hammer's face as he envisaged a further implication of the brain wave. That tasty bitch Laura, he thought—wouldn't mind getting there myself: and it'd be like doing it with Stowe looking on, his hands tied.

". . . And then there's Barbara, his ward," Stuart was saying some time later, as they ate the chops. "Nice girl. He leads her a dog's life. She got a scholarship to Cambridge a few years ago, but he worked upon her so that she never took it up. He needed her to run his house and look after him—sickening old sod. Playing on her sense of gratitude and her affection for him. The fact is, he's completely ruthless: well, I wouldn't mind that if he

didn't cover it with the most bloody awful sanctimoni-
ousness. Take an example. There was a decent bloke
who'd supplied us with certain components for donkey's
years. My uncle found this chap's son was making the
running with young Barbara. So he arranged for the
chap's factory to be flooded with orders: chap couldn't
keep his schedules, had to break his contracts, and that
was the end of him; and his son and Barbara—that was
washed up too. Oh, it happens often enough. Business
isn't a game of ring-of-roses. But what turned me up was
Uncle Herbert's subsequent sermonizing—how distress-
ing it all had been for him, but industry must be rational-
ized and superefficient nowadays if the country was to
survive. God, what crap!"

Stuart eyed Ned. Had he been piling it on a bit too
thick? The level gaze Ned returned him was not, in fact,
one of skepticism: Ned was feeling again the magnetic
pull of Stuart's personality, the spell under which he had
fallen last night: his critical judgment was in abeyance.
However, not knowing this, Stuart changed course.

"Mind you, I don't claim to be disinterested. I believe
the old man is leaving me some dough. And I'm rather
keen on Barbara myself. But I do know I could get a
fairer deal for the chaps at the works once he was out of
the way."

Stuart was rather understating the facts here. Actually
Herbert Beverley was leaving him half his fortune and
a controlling interest in the firm. Moreover, Stuart's ex-
travagance—his yacht, his Bentley, his expensive mis-
tresses—had by now got him into a very awkward spot:
he could not hold off his creditors many weeks longer.
As for Barbara, his relationship with her was very different from the one he had lightly outlined to Ned: she

could ruin him by a few words to her guardian—and she very likely would, if certain steps were not taken soon.

"Herbert's got a dicky heart," resumed Stuart. "At present, everyone but himself seems to suffer for it. Yes, he's bloody-minded all round. I've often been damn near to giving him the push. Like you and Helena. But of course I'd be the chief suspect from the start, coming in for so much money." Stuart gazed meditatively over his companion's head. "Actually, it'd be the easiest thing in the world. He's a punctuality addict: Norringham sets its watches by him. Sharp at 10:45 every night, rain, snow or earthquake, he takes his dog out for a ta-ta. A hundred yards down the road, always in the same direction, and back. One would just have to be waiting with a car, bump into him, and his dicky heart would do the rest. Fill up your glass."

Glancing at Ned, Stuart surprised a new look on his face—the thoughtful, strained look of one listening to barely audible voices in his own head.

"Your wife, now—but of course that's different; she harms nobody but you, and herself."

"We can't pretend it would be a public service to kill Helena, I agree."

Even the robust Stuart Hammer was momentarily shocked by the acrid sarcasm of Ned's remark. Talks like a bloody schoolmaster, he thought, unaware that Ned had spoken in a sudden gush of self-loathing. And, as if this had released something reckless and destructive within him, Ned continued:

"However, I'm not all that public-spirited. Let's get this quite clear, Hammer, and have no bloody hypocrisy about it—if Helena's to be put down, it'll be because *I* want her out of the way, not because she's a hopeless case, see?"

"O.K., O.K., take it easy, old son," Stuart protested, feeling as if he had turned a tap and produced a Niagara. Chap must be getting a bit tight, though I admit he's not shown the effects till now. "You live in the country, I think you told me."

"Yes. Hampshire. Converted farmhouse just outside a village. Isolated. Helena has a daily woman, but she sleeps alone when I'm away. Curious. One thing she doesn't seem to be nervy about."

"You're sure she does sleep alone?"

Ned took no offense. "Too damned sure. She's a wife on principle, a virgin by nature. If she'd only have a lover, things'd be plain sailing for me. No, she's as faithful as a burr—'faithful it seemeth, and fond, very fond, far too damnably faithful,' " he misquoted. "She trained as a professional pianist, but she used to get seized up before concerts. Don't you ever marry a failed pianist, Hammer, or you'll get the Hammerklavier played on your psyche the rest of your life."

"Let's have a spot of black coffee, old man."

When Stuart returned with the cups, he found Ned drawing a map. "Here's the house, at a bend of the lane. Nearest cottage a couple of hundred yards away, there —market garden. Lane joins road to Marksfield. Runs through a wood quarter of a mile back. There's a ride leading off the lane into the wood: good place for leaving a car, out of sight."

"Here's your coffee. Let's take this quietly, Ned. Now, supposing we come to an arrangement—"

" 'Supposing?' Isn't your heart in it? What are we doing then? Making up a fairytale?"

There was a wild, feverish look in Ned's eyes, which made Stuart Hammer uncomfortable. Things were suddenly moving too fast for his calculations: he must get them under control.

"Easy does it," he said. "It's on, then?"

"You're damn right it's on." The words came out like a cry of defiance, or despair.

"Good lad." Stuart clapped his hand on Ned's shoulder and shook it in a comradely way. "Let's get down to details."

For a couple more hours they talked. In a fortnight's time, Ned was giving a lecture about television writing to a literary society in Bristol and staying there the night. Ten days later, Stuart had a Coastal Forces reunion dinner in London. Provided Helena and Herbert Beverley stayed put on those nights—and there was no reason to suppose they would not—these seemed the most suitable dates.

Stuart now inquired closely into the Stowes' ménage. At night, according to Ned, the back door was locked: the front door had a special anti-burglar lock, but no bolts: he believed that, when he was away, Helena secured the ground-floor windows before going to bed. Her bedroom door had an old-fashioned wooden latch, and no keyhole. He drew Stuart rough plans of the house, inside and out. The Stowes did not keep a dog; but he must remember to oil the hinges of the front gate, which at present screeched abominably.

The main problem was, how should Stuart get in— "effecting an entrance, the police call it, I believe," Ned commented with an edgy laugh that made the other man look at him sharply.

"Forget the police," said Stuart. "And I don't propose

to bring a ladder on the chance that one of the upstairs windows is open. Haven't you a spare key to the front door?"

"Yes, of course, never thought of that." Ned took it off his key ring. "You'll have to leave it behind—afterward."

"Why?"

"Because, with these special burglar locks, one has to report at once if a key is lost. And the police will start asking about keys when they find the—the murderer didn't break into the house."

"What it is to be a brainworker! But of course I shall try to make it look as if someone had broken in."

"There's a secret drawer in Helena's desk. You could leave the key there."

"I'm not prodding about for secret drawers, old son—not in the small hours."

"All right. Top left-hand drawer of my chest of drawers, opposite the bedroom window. Leave it under the handkerchiefs there."

The two men continued, meticulously checking details: position of shed where ladder was kept—Stuart would leave it against the house wall to reinforce the impression that the crime had been committed by a burglar breaking in: should he actually steal anything?—no, pointless, burglar surprised by Helena loses his head, then clears out in a panic, empty-handed: position of light switches, just in case—but it would be almost full moon that night: do the stairs creak? the bedroom door?

Everything was arranged for, every contingency guarded against. One aspect alone of the problem remained untouched: by tacit consent neither man mentioned the weapon to be used upon Helena.

They turned next to the arrangements for Herbert Beverley. Stuart briefed Ned thoroughly in the appearance and habits of his prospective victim. Every night at 10:45 Herbert walked his dog, a bull terrier, into Forest Road, crossed the road, turned right, walked a hundred yards, then returned. His movements were absolutely predictable. Forest Road was a high-class residential district, its houses set well back from the road, which was fairly deserted at night, for Norringham folk went to bed early. It would be, remarked Stuart Hammer, grinning in his beard, a pushover.

"But there are street lamps, and there might be someone passing at the time. I don't like the idea of using my own car. The registration number could be spotted."

"Not unless you've switched on your lights, Ned."

"I still think it's an unnecessary risk."

Stuart frowned; then a mischievous look came on his face. "My God! Why not pinch the old man's car for the job!"

Herbert Beverley, he explained, was so mean that he would not build a garage onto his old-fashioned house, but kept his car in a cul-de-sac fifty yards away. He described the car, gave Ned its registration number, and said he would send him a key that would open it and work the ignition. Ned should leave his own car somewhere near by, and take Beverley's: if by ill luck the latter happened to be in dock that night, he would have to use his own after all.

"But couldn't you ring me up on the day if—"

"No," said Stuart. "Not on your life. The whole business depends on there having been no communication between you and me which could be traced later. The car key will come to you by post."

"But, dammit, we've got to have some means of communication in case it's necessary to postpone things. Your uncle might get flu. Helena might take it into her head to stay away from home for a night—though she very seldom does."

"All right. But I'm not having any letters or telephone calls, unless we have to alter our plans at the very last moment. Let's see now. Agony column of *The Times*'d be best. A code. You've the brain. You can spend tomorrow thinking one up."

"Actually I invented a code once, for a short story that never got written. Based on the Test averages. For instance, 'The evenings are drawing in,' inserted on the morning of the day, would mean, "All clear, go ahead.' If something goes wrong, we'd put 'The evenings are drawing out' in the Agony column."

"Fine. But where do the Test averages come in?"

"Like this. Take the final order of the batting averages. We make a list of possible messages we might have to send each other, and number them. They're keyed to the order of the England batsmen, using the first three letters of their surnames. 'Com' for Compton, 'Gra' for Graveney, and so on. May comes top in the averages: so, if you saw in the Agony column, 'The evenings are drawing out. May,' you'd look up message number one on our list and act on it."

"I'm with you. We'll work out the messages tomorrow." Stuart Hammer gave Ned the frank, jovial look which had taken in everyone but his uncle and one or two women, and said, "One thing more, old man. The question of a guarantee."

"Guarantee?"

"Yes. I'm taking first knock. I've got to be sure you'll go in when it's your turn."

"You don't trust me?" Ned was quite genuinely wounded.

"I wouldn't trust anyone but S. Hammer. Not that far, old son. I was giving the matter some thought while I was at the stove. An I.O.U.? Well, frankly, I doubt if you'd have enough money to interest me, even if Helena left you her all. So I ask myself, what's Ned standing to make out of our little transaction? Answer: his Laura. If he doesn't play *his* part, he must lose the main object of the combined operations."

"I don't—"

"What I have in mind," said Stuart, in the friendliest possible way, "just to cover myself, is that you should write a letter to your Laura—the sort of letter that'd insure she'd never wish to see you again. See what I mean? An absolutely foul missive—let yourself rip on it. You give me this letter, together with envelope addressed to her, all in your own fair hand. If you don't keep your side of the bargain I post it to her. If you do, I burn it. Neatish work, what?"

Ned was frowning. "How do I know you will burn it?" he said slowly.

"You don't," Stuart cheerfully replied. "You'll have to trust me. Well, I mean, the letter'd be useless to me once the job was done, wouldn't it?"

"Oh, yes." Ned's tone reflected a reluctance he could not account for.

Misunderstanding his hesitation, Stuart said, "It must be a *decisive* letter. And remember, you wouldn't be able to explain it to Laura afterward—not without telling her that you'd been accessory to the murder of your wife."

The appalling thing, Ned discovered when he sat down to write the letter next morning, was how easily it came to him. He was flooded with bitter resentment, previously suppressed, that Laura should be reluctant to continue as his mistress, and with suspicion rising from his knowledge of her many other affairs. He found himself even blaming her in his mind for having driven him to the desperate expedient of planning Helena's death. Everything had become so unreal for him, cut off from his past and from the outside world within the gently rocking hull of the sloop, that it seemed as if some compulsive hand were shaping the words he wrote.

Showing the letter to Stuart proved much more difficult than writing it. Ned did it with great reluctance, and with a curious embarrassment.

"Yes, this is fine as far as it goes," said Stuart crisply. "But you've forgotten that, if and when Laura received it, your wife would be dead. You must make some reference to Helena." His eye lit up. "I've got it! Put in a bit at the end saying that, since her death, you've come to realize that you loved Helena better than anyone else. That'll clinch it, coming on top of your other unkind remarks."

Ned rewrote the letter. He was then required to make a second copy, "just in case the first should get lost in the post or intercepted or anything," as Stuart Hammer meaningly put it. The rest of the day the two men spent working out their code of messages and going over their plans again and again, looking for weak spots. That evening, with Ned still immured in the cabin, *Avocet,* under her auxiliary, left the creek which Ned had never seen and set course for Yarwich.

Some five hours later, Stuart was rowing him ashore. They had hardly spoken during the voyage.

"Well," said Stuart, "our troubles will soon be over. It's all in the bag, eh?"

Ned came out of his daze. "Look here, you'll—I don't want her to suffer—you'd do it quickly?"

Stuart Hammer's lip curled a little, invisible in the darkness. "Don't you worry, old son. She won't know what's happening to her."

4   *The Snared Falcons*

THE STOWES were to have a small cocktail party this evening; and Helena was as usual in a tiz. She had not got round yet to reading Josephine Weare's new novel; Colonel Gracely only drank whisky, and half a bottle might not be enough; Ned had forgotten to bring the olives from London last night; was Lady Avening on speaking terms with Brian Holmes and his mother?

"Oh, for God's sake, Helena, don't fuss so! What does it matter?" Ned exclaimed. "Nobody expects us to entertain like millionaires."

"You'll tell me next I'm trying to keep up with the Joneses. Go on, say it." Helena's cool voice was already turning into the resentful whine he dreaded.

"I never suggested that. I'm only saying we can't afford—"

"You can afford to go off on holidays, and—and start taking *The Times.* I don't know what induces you to read the boring rag."

"And anyway, it's your money." And here we are, back in the bloody old groove again, thought Ned.

For over a week, since his return from his "Norfolk holiday," he had been trying to detach himself from Helena—to feel her as a dead woman, and accustom his palate to the exotic flavor of the idea. His half-conscious need to do so had one paradoxical effect: he found himself constantly hanging round her, unwilling to let her out of his sight. And this, misinterpreted by her, had led to one of her rare fits of amorousness. Ned remembered it now, with equal disgust and self-disgust. "Her whom abundance melts" is Laura, and "her whom want betrays" is Helena, he said to himself viciously. His mind, whirling in a vicious circle, became a stationary blur like an airplane propeller revved up. Two days more in which to make his decision. He could still send *The Times* an insertion for the Personal column—"The evenings are drawing out"—still send it tomorrow and stop Stuart Hammer. Save Helena, and ruin his own life. For a week, he realized, he had been waiting for something to happen which would force him to make this decision, for his will seemed paralyzed.

It had been like this on a previous occasion when he and Laura decided to part. They had kept away from each other for a fortnight—a period of extreme anguish for Ned—and then, their resolution failing, come together again. Their reunion had been rapturous. But, when the intoxication of it wore off, Ned felt more powerless than ever to free himself from the vicious circle in which his life ran. Even now, it was incredible to him that he should let Stuart Hammer's plan take its course. Examining himself, he realized that he was only waiting for a letter from

Laura to tell him that she would, after all, continue their relationship on the old terms.

"Why are you looking at me like that?" asked Helena.

"Sorry. I didn't know I—Like what?"

"You've been very queer since you came back from Norfolk."

"Have I? How?"

"Dreamy. Distrait. You look at me as if I was a sum that wouldn't come out."

He dreaded the intuition her oversensitivity gave her —the neurotic woman's flair for putting her finger on a man's weakest spots.

"Well, you must do your own sums, Ned," she went on, when he made no reply. She sighed. "Not that you'll ever add *me* up right. Or perhaps you think you know the answer. Well, at least you do seem to take some interest in me these days."

"I think you're a vulgar fraction posing as a compound one." He tried to say it lightly, but failed to conceal the impatience in his voice.

Helena flushed, giving her ugly shrug, and started spreading pâté on some cheese biscuits. She did it clumsily, smearing her fingers, breaking a biscuit. This clumsiness of hers, which he had found so moving when first they were in love, aroused nothing but irritation now: it was no longer even pathetic—an appeal to his tenderness. It exasperated him endlessly that so delicately formed a creature could be so maladroit, and such a slut. He looked round the room: crumbs on the floor, flowers stuffed into vases and withering, a heap of unmended socks on Helena's work table, letters—no doubt unanswered—spilling over her desk. What on earth did she do with her time? There was a thick layer of dust on the grand piano, he knew; but this he dared not even glance at, for fear of provoking an outburst of self-pity. Instead, he let his eyes rest on Helena. Thinning flaxen hair in an untidy coil on top of her head—a small head, with features delicate in profile but made lifeless by her shut-in expression; blue eyes, a little protuberant, anxious looking; slender limbs, which should have been graceful but were made angular and awkward by the unquiet spirit within.

She was a beauty once, he thought: and even now a stranger might call her attractive.

"Oh, Ned, do stop mooning around. I hate being stared at. Why don't you go and work on your play or something?"

"I'm thinking about it—rather a difficult scene."

This was a lie, of course. Living with a woman like Helena, he thought, you became infected with her self-deception: first you tempered the truth to her raw sensibility, then you were driven to dishonesty in *self-*defense.

"Have you written about that I.T.A. job yet?"

"Not yet," he replied.

"Why are you always putting things off?" she exclaimed with a stagy sigh.

Ned went cold and his face started to twitch. "Putting things off"—their conversation was always turning up these crude ironies just now. Or had Helena somehow sensed what was in his mind? The decision he must make within the next twenty-four hours? Glancing covertly at his wife, he surprised a curious expression on her face—a sly, complacent look which mystified and disturbed him. The fantastic notion crossed his mind that she did know all about it: Stuart Hammer had written and told her: Stuart was really a friend of hers, and it had been a put-up job between them so as to get Ned completely in Helena's power. That would account for Helena's not having catechized him about his Norfolk holiday—normally she'd have been on at him for hours.

Ned's brain was whirling again. With a strong effort, he slowed it down. If I live with Helena much longer, I shall become as paranoiac as she is—always suspecting plots and injuries.

"I'd better go and cut some flowers," he said.

"You needn't bother, dear. Brian Holmes left a marvelous bunch of roses at the back door this morning."

"Oh, did he? You've made a conquest."

"That's an awfully vulgar thing to say." Helena's voice stabbed like an icicle. He deliberately ignored the provocation, knowing from long experience how she hated having her provocations ignored.

"Well then, I'll empty these vases. The flowers are dead and the water stinks," he said. As he was carrying them out of the room, his wife remarked, with the petulant whine returning to her voice:

"Why are you so disagreeable about Brian?"

"Am I? He's a bit wet. Otherwise I've nothing against him."

"He does at least do a job and make a success of it."

"Unlike your ineffectual husband?" Ned spoke tonelessly, with a weary indifference which stung Helena worse than any violent answer.

"Ineffectual?" she said, then boiled over suddenly like a saucepan of milk. "Impotent is a better word. Impotent and futile! You—"

Ned left the room and shut the door on her wild ranting, lest he should be drawn into it. Misery closed down on him. He threw away the dead flowers, emptied the vases, refilled them and arranged the roses. He heard Helena banging about upstairs; making the beds—at 3 P.M.: the daily woman did not come at weekends. He wandered about downstairs, touching the furniture, the curtains, the ornaments. This was the house they had come to a few years ago, intending a fresh start; country air, the garden, fields stretching away to the wooded hills, new interests. And big, empty, farmhouse rooms for the children. But there had been no children. Better be unborn, than have a woman like Helena for a mother. Yet it might have been her salvation—who knows . . . ?

An hour later he walked down to the post office to see if any letters had come in for him by the afternoon post. There was one from Laura—the first he had received since she left him in Norfolk. To open the flimsy envelope cost him an almost superhuman effort of will, so much did he dread to know what it contained. It was a loving, despairing letter, but it removed his last hope of compromise. Laura made it quite clear that she would not resume their old relationship: he must choose between her and Helena: it was the only way out of a situation that otherwise would grow more and more intolerable. She loved him with all her heart, but about this her mind was made up.

"Your wife is looking very well," remarked Lady Avening, with the air of one who had conferred upon Mrs. Stowe this desirable condition.

"I'm glad you think so," answered Ned.

Lady Avening nodded to her husband, and her voice went into a boom like a radio suddenly turned up. "I was saying, Bob, that Mrs. Stowe looks remarkably well."

"Quite," said Sir Robert, with the start of a guilty

thing surprised. "Ah—quite. The air in this part of the world is exceptionally good. I'm sure you will find it so, Mrs. Stowe."

"Really, Bob! The Stowes have been here for years, as you well know."

"To be sure. Precisely. Old neighbors. My memory's not what—"

"My husband," Lady Avening broke in, "lives very much in the clouds."

"Like a test pilot," murmured little Josephine Weare, her enormous blue eyes fastened on Lady Avening with an entranced expression. The latter brushed it aside.

"He lives for his collection of coins. I always say it is so nice for a man to have a hobby." She inclined her head toward Mrs. Holmes. "Your son's garden, for instance. A splendid, healthy, outdoor occupation."

"But not exactly a hobby," said Mrs. Holmes dryly. "We're in market gardening for a living, you know."

"Came across an extraordinary orchid once in the Himalayas. Extraordinary," remarked Colonel Gracely. "Whopping great blue thing. Devours hummingbirds, or so the natives believe. Doesn't bear transplantation, though."

"Which is lucky for our local hummingbirds," said Josephine Weare.

"Eh? Oh, yes." The colonel peered myopically into the novelist's face. "Damned enormous blue things, Miss Weare. Like your eyes."

Josephine giggled enchantingly and the colonel beamed at her, his ascetic countenance suddenly boyish.

"You didn't actually feed hummingbirds to this orchid of yours?" she pursued.

"Well, no. I was on my way to visit a lama. Hadn't

much time for botanical investigation. I was doing some research into Tibetan dialects."

"I'm sure Colonel Gracely would not lend himself to any such barbarity," Lady Avening pronounced. "Which reminds me, Mrs. Stowe. I'm getting up an entertainment in Marksfield, for the R.S.P.C.A. funds. I want you to help us."

"Of course I will."

"I thought a few pieces on the piano would be nice."

Oh God, that's torn it, thought Ned. Helena's fists were clenched; her cool voice became a hurried gabble.

"Oh, no, I couldn't do that, I'm sorry, I'll sell tickets, address envelopes, anything you like, but not—"

"My wife never plays in public now," Ned put in. He was trying to protect Helena, but she shot a bitterly resentful glance at him. Lady Avening said:

"You shouldn't let her bury her talent in a napkin. I am a busy woman, but I have always kept up my water colors. I—"

"Music isn't a hobby for Mrs. Stowe, like—like fretwork." Brian Holmes's immature face was flushed, and his lanky frame twisted in the chair. "She's an a-a-artist, a f-first-rate c-concert pianist. You can't expect—"

"I am well aware that Marksfield is not the Albert Hall. But I'm sure, in a good cause, Mrs. Stowe would not feel it beneath her to—"

"That's not what I meant." Brian Holmes writhed, fingering his straggly beard. "It's a question of artistic integrity."

"Indeed?" Lady Avening appeared to swell within her tweeds.

"You haven't got a drink, Colonel. Let me—"

"Now you mustn't quarrel about me," said Helena.

Ned's hand, poised over the decanter, was arrested by the different note in her voice. She sounded almost gay. As long as she's the center of interest, he thought—"I gave up my career, as you all know, because I found public performances too great a nervous strain. And of course," Helena went on, "because I wanted to look after Ned. I believe a husband and a home should be a full-time job."

Lady Avening nodded approval. Her husband piped up unexpectedly:

"Rather a strain on a husband, being a full-time job."

"Really, Bob!" His spouse was roguish now. "How lucky for you that I have outside interests, then."

"Quite, m'dear."

"Marriage," said the colonel. "Hah. A good sporting gamble. Don't know why I've never tried it."

"Too many outside interests?" suggested Josephine Weare.

Mrs. Holmes remarked pleasantly, "I can recommend it, Colonel Gracely. My husband and I were very happy together."

"I often wonder, though, whether artists should marry." Helena's voice was toneless again. "What do you think, Josephine?"

"Oh, I'd take the risk. But at thirty-five I'm a bit past it."

"Nonsense, m'dear," said the colonel.

Helena ground on, like a child repeating a lesson, "It's not only that marriage endangers an artist's career. But we're such difficult people to live with. Ned could tell you. We're just a burden, with our temperaments and tantrums."

Ned recoiled inwardly. It was like Helena to play the

martyr and to point a finger so forgivingly at him as the persecutor. The atmosphere in the room felt suffocating to him: an emotional storm had been circling round, with mutters of thunder, and he almost wished it would break. He rose abruptly and began refilling glasses.

"I think," said Brian Holmes, a little too loudly, "any s-sacrifice should be m-made for art."

"What's *your* instrument? The recorder?" Ned was shocked to hear himself saying.

"Actually, I play the flute." Brian Holmes blinked at him uncertainly.

Bob Avening rubbed his hands. "Well now, why don't we have some music? Just for ourselves. Mrs. Stowe—Helena—can't I prevail upon you? It'd be a great pleasure and privilege if—"

"Oh, my wife never—" began Ned, but was astonished to see Helena get up, give him a look both defiant and sly, and open the piano.

"What shall I play?"

"Play that Schubert Impromptu," began Brian Holmes.

"I quite love Schubert," said Lady Avening. "So tuneful. Particularly *Lilac Time.*"

This is it, thought Ned. Either she'll break down in the middle or she'll never get started; she hasn't touched the instrument for years.

He was quite wrong. Helena managed very well. She had never been a flexible, still less a truly musical pianist; but, as far as Ned could tell, she was playing the right notes and all the notes. The old, brittle brilliance of her technique was recognizable, if impaired. Ned glanced round the cozy, shabby, low-ceilinged room—it had been the kitchen of the farmhouse. His six guests were clearly enjoying themselves, each in his own way; and one could hardly expect them to realize that a miracle was happening. Lady Avening gave the impression that she had been a lifelong patron of music. Her husband's eyes were closed, Josephine Weare's wide open and attentive as if she were taking notes. Colonel Gracely had his head on one side, like a bird listening. Mrs. Holmes was glancing covertly toward her son, who sprawled all over a window seat, gazing at the pianist.

Helena, after playing two Impromptus and the Liszt Petrarch Sonnet, stopped as decisively as she had begun.

"Well now, that's quite something. Thank you," said the tiny Josephine Weare. The guests all chimed in. Finally Ned, bringing his wife a drink, said:

"Well done, my dear. But I didn't know you'd been practicing."

"Oh, only when you were away, or out of the house. I know it disturbs your work."

A deadly weariness came over Ned's spirit. Helena's implication, that he was responsible for her not playing the piano—that she sacrificed everything to his comfort —sickened him. It was so cleverly, so plausibly done; and it was not true. Often in their earlier days he had tried to coax her to start playing again, but it had been useless, like all his other efforts to build her up—sooner or later she herself always knocked away the props.

He felt antagonism in the room. Helena had turned their guests against him. Mrs. Holmes alone seemed not to have been infected: her eyes conveyed some message of sympathy to him: yet the Holmeses were newcomers to the village—the other four might have been expected to know by now the true situation of things in the Stowes' ménage. God knows what Helena didn't go hinting about the place when he was away.

They were talking about television now, making efforts to bring him into the conversation; but he answered morosely, curtly. If they liked to think him surly as well as selfish, let them. A picture of Laura—generous, loving and naked—rose suddenly before his mind's eye.

Soon the guests began to disperse. Mrs. Holmes and her son went along the field path at the back which led to their cottage. The others walked down the path through the unkempt front garden. The white wicket gate screeched as Colonel Gracely opened it. I must oil that, thought Ned. Yes, of course I've got to oil it.

"I hope your lecture at Bristol goes well," called Josephine Weare as she waved good-by, her head only showing above the four-foot beech hedge.

Helena and Ned ate a scrappy supper, talking in a desultory, unreal way about their guests. Helena seemed a little tipsy, but perhaps it was still the intoxication of her recent triumph. When they had washed up, they settled down in the sitting room, Ned scribbling notes for his lecture, Helena sighing over the pile of socks she was darning. The storm, which had been circling all the evening, did not break till they were upstairs, side by side in their separate beds. Ned knew it was coming by the fidgeting of her fingers on the counterpane, and braced himself. Perhaps he could even avert it. He made a mental resolution that, if Helena showed some friendliness now, he would give up the nightmare plan in which Stuart Hammer had involved him, though it would mean losing Laura forever.

"It was marvelous to hear you playing again," he forced himself to say.

Her fingers plucked the counterpane furiously. "Really? Why did you grudge me my little success then?"

"*Grudge* you? Helena—"

"You sulked all the rest of the time they were here. It was too painfully obvious. You can't bear anyone else getting the limelight for a moment."

"You know that's nonsense. I was annoyed, I admit, because you made them think I prevented you from practicing."

"And you were unpardonably rude to Brian Holmes."

"That's it! Change the subject when you're in the wrong!"

"Don't shout at me, Ned. My nerves won't stand it. Brian does do a decent job, anyway, and sticks at it."

"When he's not mooning over you." A sudden thought struck Ned. What had Brian said—"Play that Schubert Impromptu." "I suppose it's him you've been playing to while I was away."

"Why not? At least he's interested in me."

"I wish you luck of him. Have you dragged him into bed yet?"

"Don't be so unutterably cheap. The role of jealous husband doesn't suit you. You've forfeited any right to—"

"So you *have!*"

"Your elation is premature. I have not been to bed with Brian. And I've no intention of doing so: it would give you just the excuse you want."

"Excuse? What on earth—?"

"For wallowing about with whatever bitch you're sniffing after just now. And with a clear conscience."

Ned's whole body was shaking uncontrollably. Two feet away, Helena lay rigid and pale in the moonlight that streamed through the low window. Without having to look at her, he knew the expression on her face: gratification. She loved whipping him out of control, she fed upon the signs that showed her destructive power over him. Now is the moment to tell her about Laura, he thought. Now or never. And he knew it would be never, because—beneath his exasperation, his loathing and pity for this woman—he was afraid of her. He made a strenuous effort to master himself.

"Look, Helena. We simply cannot go on like this. I've —we've both tried. It's hopeless."

"You want to get rid of me, don't you?" She gave a gusty dramatic sigh. "I've never been much use to you, I know."

Ned hardened himself against the old self-pitying appeal. "We're neither of us any use to each other. Why don't we admit it, and—"

"Yes?" Her voice was at once deadly quiet. "And what?"

"And separate."

"You have someone else in mind? I hope she can support you in the style to which I've accustomed you."

"I've no one 'in mind,'" Ned angrily, miserably retorted, knowing he had failed again. He could not face the fury Helena would become if he told her about Laura. Out of his humiliation, he went on more viciously, "I'm bored with you, bored with your dishonesty and schoolgirl sarcasm. What I have in mind is to preserve my own sanity."

Helena's legs kicked convulsively under the bedclothes.

"And don't stage one of your fits of hysterics," Ned shouted. "They don't impress me any longer."

His wife's voice went into a muttering gabble, low, leaden and monotonous. "You'd like me dead, wouldn't you, wouldn't you? But you haven't the nerve to kill me. Go on kill me go on I dare you here I am hit me then hit me! You see? You can't you're not a man you can't touch me you can't make love to me you can't even be unfaithful no woman would look at you except some filthy whore filthy whore filthy—"

Ned was out of bed, slapping her hard on both cheeks. "For Christ's sake pull yourself together and shut up!"

Her stone eyes hated him from the pillow. Then the new, sly look returned to them. She kicked away the bedclothes, tore off her nightdress, and staring at Ned exclaimed:

"I'm giving you one last chance."

"You're giving *me*—" He bit off the rest of it. "Chance of what?"

"You know." Her thin, pallid body trembled. Her voice coolly mocked him now. "To be a husband. Take me or leave me, I shall never let you go—you hear?— never. So you might as well have the benefit of me."

This was worse, far worse, than it had ever been. Ned felt flayed all over. "Cover yourself up," he said coldly. "You're not an attractive sight."

He got back into bed. The faint, sweet, clean smell of grassland came through the open window on a breeze that stirred the curtains. The springs of compassion, of mercy, were dried up within him forever, he felt. He heard Helena's voice going on and on, as it had done so often before, dredging up grievance after grievance from the past, vindictively exposing his own weaknesses, holding up for inspection every inch of the tattered fabric of their relationship. But tonight this terrible cadenza left him cold. Helena had lost her power to drag him into the maelstrom of her own mind: the recent scene had finally destroyed the last link between them. He hardly heard what she was saying now. Other words kept beating in his head—"I shall never let you go . . . I shall never let you go."

She was lying on her back, silent at last, her face like a death mask in the moonlight. A mousy smell pervaded the room. Ned saw her rigid, sculptured form shaping the bedclothes into folds of light and shadow. He saw her as the effigy of a woman, a dead woman, the dead woman she soon would be.

5   *The Upright Director*

SELF-CONFIDENCE, which had been the making of Stuart Hammer, might well prove his undoing. At times he carried it—or it carried him—to the lengths of abnormal vanity and perilous complacence. He had been saved, so far, because his distrust of others was in proportion to his trust in himself. This Sunday morning, while Ned Stowe still slept, exhausted by the scene with Helena, Stuart was giving him considerable thought. The fellow had nerve, no doubt of that, in an emergency: but had he the stamina? He was desperate enough to want his wife got rid of. But there was a softness in him, Stuart reckoned, which might wreck their scheme. The chap was a bit off balance—the type who would follow you boldly enough into action: would you choose him, though, for a solitary mission? And unless Ned did his stuff when his turn came, it would be the bottom of the ladder again for Stuart.

Since joining his uncle's firm, Stuart had rapidly stepped up his standard of living. At present he occupied a couple of rooms in a country club just outside Norringham—a flashy place where no questions were asked and where credit was unlimited, for a certain period: that period, for Stuart, was drawing to its close, even though he had done the proprietor—the usual "Major, retd."—a number of what in business circles are called "favors."

Stuart glanced at his gold Cartier wrist watch, rang down to the restaurant for a large breakfast, put on a heavy silk monogrammed dressing gown, washed and shaved, then sauntered into his sitting room. This he had furnished himself: deep crimson-leather armchairs and settee, television set, cocktail cabinet, hunting prints on the maroon walls, an outsize desk—its drawers filled with bills—a round inlaid rosewood table, and an array of gadgets for making life comfortable. Stuart Hammer did not surround himself with luxurious and pretentious objects, as many men do who have no time or capacity for the private life, in order to bolster himself up: he did it because of a firm conviction that he had a right to such things.

Drawing the curtains, Stuart Hammer looked out over the regimented "grounds" of the club toward the factory chimneys and spires of Norringham beyond. He drew a deep breath. There was the Beverley works; and Beverley's was Norringham: if all went well, Stuart Hammer would soon be Beverley's. An early couple strolled, swinging their rackets, past the beds of geranium and lobelia, toward the hard court.

The door opened. A blonde came in, carrying a large tray, and began setting the table. Stuart ran his eye over her like a cattle dealer; she was new to the place—the casualty rate among the maids at the country club was high, but its proprietor never had much difficulty over replacements.

"Day of rest, Peggy?"

"Not for me, Mr. Hammer."

"No rest for the wicked, eh?"

"Wicked? Me?" The girl tossed her head affectedly.

"I hope so. Just a little. I like naughty girls, and they like me."

Peggy wiggled her haunches, at which Stuart Hammer was staring, and pretended indignation.

"Well, I'm not then, Mr. Hammer."

"Stuart to you, darling."

She gave him a bold, provocative look, which he returned with such interest that her loose mouth fell half open.

"You have a cheek, I must say," she replied, a little breathlessly, turning away.

"I've got what it takes. And so have you. We should get together sometime."

"What a hope!"

"Trouble is, I sleep badly. Have to take a sleeping draught every night."

"So what?"

"No use unless a pretty nurse gives it to me. Doctor's prescription."

"You find someone else then."

"Come here, Peggy."

"I've work to do. And your coffee's getting cold."

"Oh, that won't do." His hard blue eyes locked with hers. "I like it hot. And sweet. Well, off you go to your Sunday school," he added in a mincing voice.

"Ta-ta now, Mr. Hammer."

"Stuart."

"Stuart."

"I have to be given my sleeping draught sharp at 11 P.M."

A pushover, he thought. He began to devour his large breakfast, glancing at the Sunday papers. Things were boiling up all right in the Middle East. Just how long could he keep Meyer on the string? If the deal went through, there'd be a tidy sum in his sock, and the prospect of more to come. Meyer would divert the shipment to his Arab chums: the cover was absolutely foolproof—safe as houses. If only that dried-up prig Herbert Beverley were not so obstinate and suspicious. Herbert did not trust Meyer. Well, what the hell was that to do with business? Meyer was good for his commitments—not even Herbert disputed it. Who cared where the stuff went as long as it was paid for?

It maddened Stuart that he still had no official say in the firm's policy. And now it looked as if he'd exaggerated to Meyer his personal influence with his uncle. Well, he'd give the old fool one last chance. After lunch today. And there was the little matter of Barbara, too. Herbert's niece and ward had been another iron in the fire for Stuart, and he'd be damn near burning himself on her if he wasn't careful. He supposed he could always marry her, in the last resort. But God forbid!

The brush with Peggy and the large breakfast, however, had soon restored Stuart Hammer's self-confidence. He finished reading the papers, dressed at leisure, then took the new Bentley for a spin over the flat country south of Norringham. At 12:45 he drew up outside his uncle's house. Herbert Beverley's black Humber stood in the cul-de-sac down the road opposite. Stuart eyed it, fingering an ignition key in his pocket.

Barbara opened the door to him. A white bull terrier at her side scrutinized him without any marked enthusiasm. He gave Barbara a cousinly kiss, which she did not return, and followed her into a small sitting room on the left of the gloomy hall. Turning to face him—a tall, angular girl in tweed skirt and magenta-colored sweater, wearing no make-up—she said:

"Well, Stuart, your worries are over."

"What's that? Oh, I see. I'm very glad, darling."

"It was a false alarm."

"Good girl." He smacked her lightly on the bottom. "But you gave me a hell of a fright."

"No doubt," she dryly answered. "I can imagine the prospect of having to marry me must have alarmed you terribly."

"Oh, damn it, Babs, don't talk like a schoolmarm," said Stuart, irritable with relief.

The girl turned away. She disliked Stuart's sensual patronizing, disliked being called "Babs"—though it had sounded sweet enough during the brief period of her infatuation for this man. To one brought up in the cultivated but rather strait-laced and humorless ménage of Herbert Beverley, Stuart had seemed at first an exotically attractive personality. His buccaneering air, his flashy spending, his brassy effrontery in love-making had appealed to the inexperienced girl as a merry-go-round at a fair might appeal to an overprotected child. Barbara had been lifted off her feet, whirled round and round, then the whole thing had ground to a stop, and her natural good sense told her how garish it had all been. She was lucky to have paid so lightly for her ignorance and folly, she thought, catching sight of Stuart Hammer's face in the mirror before her—a pudgy, pinkish, complacent face which, without the beard and the eyeshade, Ned Stowe would not have recognized.

"Are you trying to tell me that our understanding—that we're washed up?"

Turning, the girl faced him squarely. "What understanding?"

"There was an agreement, you may remember, that we should get married, as soon as—"

"As soon as it was certain I was going to have your child? Well, I'm not. So that's that."

"My dear girl, what on earth's the matter with you? Don't you want to marry me? You were keen enough last time we met."

Stuart should not have added that final phrase, but he felt genuinely aggrieved. For Barbara, it snapped the last remaining link.

"I've no wish to marry you at all," she said, more loudly than she had intended. She bent down to pat the dog and hide her flushed cheeks, so she did not see Stuart's fists clenching. A cold anger had possessed him, directed not only against the girl but against Herbert Beverley, whose mannerisms and donnish habit of speech she often unconsciously reproduced. It was one thing to learn that he need not marry Barbara, and quite a different thing to be shown so unequivocally that she had no desire to marry him. Stuart Hammer's sexual vanity was not accustomed to taking such knocks. His immediate response was typical of the man: striding forward, he fastened his arms round Barbara and his mouth on hers.

"Still not want me?" he said.

"No, Stuart," she replied, quite coolly. "You overestimate your fascination."

His immensely strong fingers dug into her soft shoulders. She gasped, and the bull terrier began to snarl fiercely. As Stuart Hammer stepped back, the door opened and Herbert Beverley came in.

"Well, Stuart! Sorry I was not down to welcome you. I've had a poor night. I hope Barbara has been entertaining you."

"I'm sorry to hear that, sir. Yes, Barbara and I have been having a chat," replied Stuart, with the manly deference which he always assumed toward his uncle. And if I tore dear Barbara's clothes off and put her on the floor, he savagely thought, you would have a heart attack and die saying "Tut-tut, Stuart, you are forgetting yourself."

Ned Stowe would certainly have recognized Herbert Beverley from the physical description Stuart had given him. Herbert was a small, spare old man, still very erect in carriage; he wore a black, lay-reader's kind of suit; the eyes behind the pince-nez showed a lively interest in what they saw, though the dark pouches beneath them told their tale. He spoke precisely, pedantically at times, in a not unmelodious voice, and all in all might easily have been mistaken for the old-fashioned type of Sixth Form classical tutor. There was a severity about him, indeed; but it came from his deep, rigorous idealism, not from any meanness of spirit. He was a liberal and nonconformist of the old school, a model employer, an indulgent guardian to Barbara, and a man of keenly analytical intelligence who could have been equally successful in many other walks of life—in fact, the reverse of the domestic tyrant and ruthless tycoon whom Stuart had pictured for Ned Stowe.

Unfortunately for Herbert, though he had few illusions about his nephew, his idealism disqualified him from seeing really deep into Stuart Hammer. He believed that every man is capable of improvement. He had given Stuart a responsible job in the conviction that responsibility would steady him, bring out the best in him, and would never have admitted there was no best to bring out. Stuart was doing well enough in the job: but, even if he had done less well, Herbert would have stood by him, for his Victorian family feeling made it unthinkable that Beverley's should pass into the control of anyone else as long as there was Beverley flesh and blood available. It was Herbert's dream that Stuart and Barbara should prolong the Beverley dynasty. He had thrown them together, and looked for the signs of an understanding between them; the eyes behind the pince-nez lost their shrewdness when, as now, he was observing these two.

At lunch, Barbara was more than usually silent. Stuart Hammer, who always felt oppressed by the huge dining table, the Georgian silver, the somber Dutch oil paintings, and the parlormaid, whose starched Victorian cap and apron consorted so ill with her slovenly Midland speech, tended to show off on these occasions. He was telling them how, during his recent sailing holiday, he had by skillful seamanship averted a collision with a cargo liner at night. From this, he moved on to certain war episodes in which he had figured prominently. The disabused look in Barbara's eye was a challenge; Stuart still had no doubt he could bring her to heel again, if and when he wanted. Herbert Beverley, on the other hand, listened with an almost childlike raptness. Delicate health had always prevented him from taking part in active physical pursuits; and, though Stuart did not realize this, it was the adventurer in him which appealed to his uncle most. From time to time, Herbert glanced at his ward: but, if she was feeling any Desdemona-like response to Stuart's tales of "moving accidents," she showed no signs of it.

"Barbara seems rather distrait lately," said the old man, when he had taken Stuart into his study after lunch. "I hope there is nothing wrong between you."

"Wrong? How do you mean?" It annoyed Stuart that with his uncle he should so often find himself behaving like a schoolboy on the defensive.

"My dear boy, I have always hoped that you two would come to an understanding," said Herbert in his melodious, rather fluting voice. "And recently it did seem that you were interested in each other. However, I have no wish to force you into confidences, if—"

"Quite, sir, quite. Babs is a fine girl. But perhaps she is too young yet to know her own mind."

"I doubt if women are ever too young to know when they are in love," replied Herbert Beverley, with a dryness of irony which frequently disconcerted his nephew.

"Well, you know, she's lived a sheltered life, and I've always been a rolling stone."

"Are you suggesting," said Herbert with a twinkle, "that contrast of experience makes for incompatibility in marriage?"

Stuart was nettled, but strove to conceal it. "I'm afraid I don't know much about marriage. I'm only saying that maybe I'm not Babs's type."

"And who would you say *is* her type?"

"Oh, I dunno. Someone more like yourself, perhaps."

"A safe, hard-working, dry old stick, eh? I don't think you can know much about women, my boy, if that's what you believe."

Stuart frowned. Not know much about women, indeed! He could tell the old fool a thing or two about Babs that would knock him off his perch.

"Well," said Herbert, "we must let that lie on the table for a while. Now, I'd like your views on another matter. I've been thinking of modifying our pension scheme for the office staff. With the falling value of money, it seems to me that our present arrangements are not altogether satisfactory."

They discussed the matter for some time. Stuart Hammer, who saw himself taking over a controlling interest in the firm before long, did not at all wish to be saddled with higher contributions to the staff's pensions. On the other hand, his reluctance must be carefully concealed, for his uncle's good will toward him depended partly upon Stuart's assumed interest in the welfare of their employees.

"It's a question of our profit margin, I suppose, sir. Of course, I don't pretend to be an authority on the financial side. But raw-material costs are likely to go on rising, and wages won't stay pegged at their present level. Unless we can increase the gross profits—"

"And how would you propose to do that?" asked Herbert, with the quizzical look of a don listening to a not overtalented pupil reading an essay. This was, of course, Stuart's opportunity; he had worked for it, he thought, rather neatly.

"Well, there's Meyer's proposal, for instance. He'll take as much as we can supply, and he's definitely willing to offer ten per cent above what we get from any of our established clients. I believe we could bump him up to fifteen per cent."

"Why?"

"Why? Sorry, sir, I don't get you."

"Why is Meyer willing to cut his own profits? That's what it amounts to. From what I know of him, it doesn't sound at all in character."

"Presumably he's got a good market for the stuff lined up."

"In the Middle East?"

Stuart Hammer shrugged. "I wouldn't know. Does it matter? We're not in business for our health."

"That's a phrase which always puzzles me," said Herbert mildly. "Our health is just what we *are* in business for, I should have thought—ours, and our employees'. And the country's."

"If we don't supply Egypt with the stuff, Russia will collar the market. I call it a patriotic—"

"So it *is* Egypt?"

Stuart bit his lip, looking surly. Herbert continued:

"And you consider it would be a patriotic action to let Egypt and the Arab countries have our components so that they can broadcast more effectively their propaganda against Israel—and against Britain? My dear Stuart, you are altogether too subtle for me."

"The Yids have had it coming to them for years."

"What a pugnacious chap you are!" said Herbert, with a smile which his nephew misinterpreted as a sign of yielding. Encouraged, he went on to paint a highly colored picture of the Beverley products winning a monopoly over the whole of the Middle East. "We break into a new market, which is capable of great expansion. We rake in the profits. We can increase the pensions and other amenities for our employees," he concluded.

"I see. Yes." Herbert Beverley gave Stuart a frosty glance through the pince-nez, and his small mouth primmed. "And what do *you* make out of all this, Stuart?"

"Me? If the firm prospers, I prosper."

"I mean, how much is Meyer going to slip you if the contract goes through?"

Stuart was too astute to bluster a denial. Anyway, it was too late now. He assumed the gay buccaneer personality, for which he knew his uncle had a soft spot.

"Oh, I shan't lose by it. Meyer will see to that," he said with a rollicking laugh.

"It's lucky someone in this firm has some morals. But leaving aside the morality of it, your scheme is a wildcat—"

"Meyer is good for his commitments," protested Stuart.

"I daresay. And good for nothing else. My poor boy, you're an innocent in these matters. Let me tell you a little about Meyer." Herbert Beverley proceeded to do so, revealing a detailed knowledge about the enterprising Mr. Meyer's practices and associations which quite alarmed Stuart. Stung by being called "an innocent," he lost some of his veneer of deference.

"You can't tell me you've never done business with any man who has overstepped—"

"When I do business with crooks," Herbert icily interrupted, "I make sure it's they and not I who suffer for it."

"Well then, do business with Meyer and let him suffer."

"How much money do you need, my boy?" The unexpectedness of the question took Stuart utterly aback.

"Need? I'm all right!" he stammered, forgetting for a moment the manly-frankness line he had set for himself.

"To pay off your creditors," pursued the old man,

with gentle remorselessness. "A thousand? Five thousand?"

Stuart realized that he had only to say the word, and his uncle's family pride would foot the bill. But he could not say it. How often, as a boy, he had sat like this while his father catechized him about his pocket money, making him give an account of every penny he had spent. Now he was seething with the same humiliation and sullen anger. His father and this uncle were the only two people who had the power to demolish Stuart's image of himself, to make him feel small—and he hated Herbert with the rancor he had once felt for his father.

"You can't live on your salary at the rate you do live, my dear boy. I haven't spoken to you about this before, but it's beginning to be talked about in Norringham, and that doesn't do the firm any good."

"I can manage perfectly well, thank you," Stuart stonily replied.

His uncle raised a hand in a gesture of resignation, suddenly looking more than his seventy years. "I have always believed you to be honest," was all he said. Stuart, with his detestable flair for spotting human weakness, at once heard the appeal in Herbert's voice, and saw how frail were the old man's defenses. His confidence came flooding back. He spoke lightly, almost contemptuously.

"You needn't worry about me. I can look after myself. I don't want charity; but it's a bit riling when I bring business to the firm and you won't even look at the proposition."

Herbert Beverley rose from his chair and stood very erect, tapping his pince-nez on Stuart's lapel. "No, Stuart. I appreciate your efforts on the firm's behalf, but let this be understood—under no circumstances will I touch Meyer, and as long as I am head of the firm my policy decisions are to be obeyed."

"So that's that. Very well." Stuart Hammer went up on the balls of his toes, adding, "I hope you won't live to regret it." He could not help smiling. Herbert Beverley would *not* live, either to regret this decision or to see it justified.

6 *The Faithless Wife*

FOR NED STOWE, the next three days were a
desert. Time seemed to be clogged, crawling from minute to minute, crawling like a slug and leaving behind it
a long smear over the memory, so that he could hardly
recollect what he had been doing a day or an hour before. They had eaten, then had slept; in a meaningless
way they had talked. Helena was in a strange mood; or
perhaps it was his own mood—the necessity to keep his
heart hardened, not so much against her as against the
implications of what was now irrevocable—that made
her seem so strange.

Twice he had been almost shaken out of his unnatural
calm. At breakfast on Monday, reading the paper,
Helena exclaimed, "How extraordinary!"

"Oh, what's that?"

"Here's a woman who killed her husband in their
bedroom, and locked the door, and went on living in the
house for a week afterward, having friends in to parties."

"She must have been mad," said Ned dully, in order

to say something, in order not to say that it was even more extraordinary to share a house with a *living* corpse.

On Tuesday, Helena found something else in a newspaper deserving of comment. Glancing down to the Personal column of *The Times,* she remarked:

"Here's a cryptic note. *The evenings are drawing in.* What do you make of that?"

"I don't make anything of it. In the Personal column, is it? A nice change from *Lady of title wishes to dispose of her fourth-best mink,* anyway."

"Don't criminals communicate with one another in code like this?"

"So they say."

"And clandestine lovers?"

"Probably."

"How much does it cost?"

"How the hell should I know?" Ned was seized with alarm. The receipt for the postal order he had sent—it might arrive while he was away, Helena might open it and put him through one of her suspicious questionings.

No, of course, she would be dead before he got back from Bristol.

He had watched her eating a hearty breakfast. There was a suppressed excitement about her which he could not account for, unless it was a projection of his own state of mind. The horror of Sunday night, all the mud which had been stirred up then, seemed to have subsided and left her crystal-clear, sparkling. Perhaps these outbursts, so hideous to him, were therapeutic for her. His eyelids still felt leaden, and his skin crawled as if it had bred vermin.

For the last two days, Ned had suffered continuously from indigestion. At dinner tonight, catching Helena's eye fixed upon him with a curious, speculative expression, he suddenly conceived the notion that she was poisoning him. It would be a wonderfully ironic situation. Some slow poison: arsenic probably. She was *capable de tout*. Why, otherwise, this unusual solicitude for his health? Yesterday, when the pain had been so bad that he distractedly told her he couldn't face the idea of going to Bristol, she had urged him to take a double dose of his indigestion cure, and had prepared it for him herself. A white powder. Like arsenic. But didn't arsenic have a bitter taste? Ned felt a mounting panic, and pushed away his plate of veal.

"Sorry, I just can't eat any more. It's this foul indigestion."

"You really should see a doctor, my dear."

"Perhaps I'll go to one in Bristol, if it doesn't get better."

"Are you sure you oughtn't to cancel your lecture?" Helena asked with an anxious look.

"Oh, no. I can't possibly. It's too late now."

"Well, don't forget to pack your indigestion powder."

A physical and spiritual nausea racked him the whole evening. After an almost sleepless night, he dragged himself out of bed, shaved, packed, tried to swallow some toast and coffee. He had arranged to drive to London and catch a Bristol train from Paddington; that way, Helena at least would not be able to use the car if she should take it into her head at the last moment to go somewhere else for the night. Ned felt a strong revulsion now from this planning.

"Look here, why not drive me into Marksfield for the London train?"

"But you decided—"

"You might want to use the car yourself, this afternoon or—"

"You're very thoughtful all of a sudden, Ned." She spoke without sarcasm, in a distrait manner. "No thanks, I shall put in a few hours on the piano."

"Oh, good."

Oh God, he thought. Oh God, oh God! Well, she's had her chance. She's had chances enough. I've turned myself inside out, all these years, trying to make a go of it, trying to help her. I can do no more. I'm broken up, nearly done for. I could not save her. I must save what's left of myself.

Their parting was, under the circumstances, almost farcically an anticlimax. Helena, her faded golden head averted, put up a cheek for him to kiss. He could not bring himself to do this, but patted her cheek gently instead, then hurried out to the shed where the car was kept. As he drove past the white wicket gate, he saw her standing there, waving wildly to stop him and holding up in the other hand the bottle of indigestion powder which he had, after all, omitted to pack. He drove on, accelerating hard, to put her behind him, far behind him, out of sight. Out of her misery.

The drive to London was a jumble of sharp, disconnected impressions. Ned pushed the car along at top speed, as if he were being pursued, fighting it round the bends, fighting off the thought which clamored on the threshold of consciousness. Avoiding by a hairsbreadth a collision at one blind corner, he found himself quite unshaken: a strange, old-soldier's fatalism, like oil on water, was spreading over his troubled mind. The situation, being out of his control now, seemed outside his responsibility too, as though Helena were in the last

stages of some incurable disease which he might deplore
but could not remedy.

A telephone booth at the London garage, where he put
his car, reminded him that he could still ring Helena, still
warn her; but the current of what he felt as destiny carried him past it without a struggle. In the train, a white-
faced, dull-eyed man to his fellow travelers, Ned took
out the thought which he had been suppressing and faced
it squarely. I, Edwin Stowe, who have never done any
great harm to anyone, am—shall be in fourteen hours or
so—a murderer. A cowardly murderer, not even capable
of striking the blow for himself. The accusation, he discovered, left him cold: his intelligence no longer
squirmed to evade it: there was not the faintest cry from
his conscience. On the contrary, the fact that he made a
decision, appalling though the decision was, gave him a
feeling of positive exhilaration. He had ended the stale-
mate, broken the vicious circle. No doubt he was
damned; but he felt—only one word for it—reborn. The
old Ned was as remote as Helena. What would Laura
think of the new Ned? What would she say if she knew
how he had come into being?

Stuart Hammer's thoughts, as he drove southward that
night, were of an entirely practical nature. He believed
he had guarded against nearly all foreseeable contingen-
cies. He had decided not to use the Bentley since, even
with the false number plates he possessed—relics of an
earlier lawless enterprise—a Bentley might call attention
to itself and be remembered. To hire a car might conceiv-
ably land him in other complications. The problem had
been solved by a brilliant piece of opportunism on his
part. A week ago, drinking at the bar of the country club

with a fellow resident, he had got into an argument on one of the few subjects which seemed to him worthy of controversy—women. He was soon boasting of his exploits in this field, whereupon his companion, becoming justifiably irked, remarked that anyone who owned a Bentley could pick up any girl he liked—in Norringham, at any rate—and if Stu-boy thought it was his alleged charm and potency that did the trick, he'd better think again. Stu-boy did some rapid thinking at this point, the upshot of which was that he offered to lend the bloke his Bentley for a couple of nights next week, and laid him £10 that, even with this aid, he would fail to make any impression on Peggy, the new blonde wench at the club. The bet had been taken, and the other man agreed to lend Stuart his own car in exchange, a nondescript-looking 12 h.p. sedan, during the nights in question.

"But don't let on to anyone, old man," Stuart said. "My uncle would foam at the mouth if this sort of thing got round to him."

"O.K. But if I make the wench, which of course I shall, how shall I be able to prove it to you?"

"*Prove* it? I hope we're gents, old man. I'd take your word for it. But you won't get near her, believe you me."

On the Sunday night, Stuart Hammer had insured that the girl Peggy should have no interests outside himself for a while: indeed, she was quite dazed with love for him and might soon prove an embarrassment.

However, he had no thoughts to spare for her now, as he drove the nondescript-looking sedan through the night. He wore gloves, an old blue suit, rubber-soled shoes, a dark overcoat, a cloth cap and night-driving glasses. In the overcoat pocket were an electric torch, a blackjack, and the key to the Stowes' front door. Stuart went over the drill again in his mind. At Marksfield, take the Portsmouth road; three miles out of Marksfield, turn right at signpost for Crump End; go down this lane for about three-quarters of a mile, then turn left into woodland ride. Switch off lights, substitute false number plates, lock car doors, walk out of wood down lane another quarter mile. White wicket gate on right, brick path to front door . . .

Stuart Hammer's plan was to kill the Stowe woman straight away. He would then open the bedroom window, if it were not already open, go downstairs and out by the front door, fetch the ladder from the shed at the back of the house, and climb in through the bedroom window: this would enable him to leave signs of burglarous entry. He would then knock over a chair or two, to suggest there had been a struggle (assuming, of course, that there had not in fact been one), and pocket any valuables he found lying about. Climbing down the ladder again, he would throw the valuables into a flower bed, so as to give the impression the burglar had lost his nerve after being surprised by Mrs. Stowe and killing her, and had discarded these evidences of his crime.

Climbing up and down the ladder seemed the most dangerous part. He would be visible from the lane, the moon being full. Ned had told him this lane carried little traffic, and at 1 A.M. there should be nobody stirring. It was a small risk, but a real one.

The contingency, Stuart reflected, which he could not provide for was his accomplice's letting him down. The go-ahead message had appeared in *The Times*, certainly, but only at the last moment. Had there been some hitch in Ned's arrangements? And, still more important, how accurate was the information he had given Stuart about his house and about Helena's habits? Could it be relied on? Ned was a scatterbrained chap, and halfway round the bend—the sort who might easily be wrong about some quite crucial detail. Suppose, for instance, that the Stowe woman did in fact bolt her front door as well as lock it when her husband was away? Well, he'd just have to ring the bell, get her out of bed, tell her his wife had been taken ill in the car outside and ask if he could telephone a doctor. Once he had a foot in the house, it'd be all right. But the procedure might then be rather clumsy and messy.

However, thought Stuart, there was no use anticipating the worst; one should count one's blessings: the night was fine and dry, the car running well, and with any luck he should be back at the country club before anyone was up. The 120-mile drive was nearly finished. Oxford and Reading were behind him. He passed through Marksfield at 12:40 A.M., well up to schedule, took the left fork by the Town Hall, and sped away on the Portsmouth road.

Rounding a bend a mile outside the town, his headlights picked up a car in the ditch just ahead, and a man in the road holding up his arms. Stuart accelerated, and the man reeled aside, cursing: he was evidently tight, and no doubt he would have been temporarily blinded by Stuart's headlights. But there was just a chance he might have read the rear number plate. This little contretemps was enough to throw Stuart into the cold, brutal rage which obstacles in his path always generated. He had decided not to change the number plates till he reached his destination, in case he should be involved in an accident or a police check en route, but it seemed a mistake now.

In three minutes, he was driving slowly down the winding lane to Crump End. The beam of his headlights jerked from tree trunk to tree trunk of the wood to his left. Presently the low bank between road and wood stopped short. Stuart did not immediately turn into the ride. He had worked out a drill and he was not altering it. Switching off the headlamps, he took a couple of petrol tins from the trunk and refilled the tank: that took care of the journey back. He then walked away up the drive, shining his electric torch before him.

Twenty paces into the wood he stopped, listening intently. A strongish wind had got up, and boughs were creaking together overhead like the grinding of teeth. Apart from this, and an occasional rustle in the undergrowth, there was no sound. Stuart sniffed the mushroomy, decaying smell of the wood. Damp. He walked on another thirty paces, to find the drive descending quite sharply. If he brought his car this far, the slope would hide it from the lane; but unfortunately the grass surface of the drive became wetter and more slippery here, and he might get bogged down trying to start the car uphill when he left.

"Why the hell didn't that fool tell me the place was a bloody bog?" he muttered to himself, with another spurt of anger.

Returning to the car, he substituted the false number plates which had been hidden under the rear seat, and backed slowly into the drive, stopping just before the point where it began to slope downward. He had taken off his gloves to alter the number plates; and now, getting out of the car, he stumbled in a deep rut, and throwing out a hand for support, found himself gripping a bramble while another bramble branch slashed viciously across his

cheek, and his cap was torn off his head. He fumbled for
a handkerchief, mopped at his bleeding hand and face;
he was tight with rage now, compressed like a spring.
Locking the car, he threw a rug over the hood, tapped
his overcoat pockets, and set off down the drive. There
was a flask of brandy in the dashboard recess, but Stuart
felt no need for it now. Afterward, perhaps.

Standing in the lane, he could only just pick out the
dark bulk of the car. The rug covered the chromium
fittings on the hood which would have caught the moonlight. No one passing along the lane would notice the
car, fifty paces away down the woodland drive, unless he
stopped and looked hard for it.

After listening for a minute—though footsteps could
hardly have been heard, if anyone else was abroad tonight, against the rush of wind through trees and hedges
—Stuart Hammer began to walk rapidly, with his purposeful, rolling gait, down the lane toward Crump End.
There were no more qualms in his mind than in the mind
of a tiger approaching a drinking pool. Would the quarry
be there?—that was his single thought.

He walked at the side of the road, where there was a
deep ditch, stopping every fifty yards to listen and peer
ahead. The wood on his left fell behind him; the moonlight glimmered over fields, like a heavy dew, and presently it revealed a long, low house, unlighted, ahead of
him to his right. This must be it. Yes, a white wicket gate.
THE OLD FARM.

Crouching behind the low hedge, one hand on the
gate, Stuart Hammer looked up. That was the window.
Something fluttered there. A curtain. The window was
open. Fine. He pressed the latch and pushed the gate
very slowly away from him. The hinges made no sound,

which he took as a good omen—Ned had oiled them, good old Ned hadn't forgotten. Silently he closed the gate behind him, glanced up again at the open window; and then, after this slow-motion business, covered the twenty yards between gate and front door with the soundless, darting celerity of a cat chasing a leaf.

He was in shadow now, beneath a shallow porch. A heady smell of tobacco plants came to his nostrils. He inserted the key in the lock; the solid oak door made no resistance, opening under the light pressure of his shoulder. He shone his torch beam into the black, gaping throat of the hall. Empty. He slipped in, closing the door behind him and releasing the catch of the lock. The faint click this made, as if it were the start of a chain reaction, merged into a hoarse, strangulated, rasping sound, which set his heart bumping. He swung round in the darkness to face whatever the thing was. And the next instant, a grandfather clock, which had been gathering its senile forces to strike, began chiming the hour.

Under cover of the sound, Stuart Hammer, his nerve perfectly restored, darted up the staircase, following his torch beam like a bulky shadow. Turn right on the landing, Ned had told him, then it's the first door on the right. Breathing evenly, Stuart marked the position of the wooden latch and stowed the torch away in his overcoat pocket. It was dark as a cupboard now. He advanced both hands to the latch, and with immense caution very slowly depressed it.

The door, which he pushed open inch by inch, gave one loud creak and one only. There was a sound of breathing, arrested and then continuing; Stuart thought it must be his own, till he realized he had been holding his breath. Something trickled down his cheek—sweat, or blood from the bramble scratch. He felt unpleasantly hot in his heavy overcoat; he should have left it in the hall. There was a faint smell of human warmth and of sweat, carried by the draft from the open bedroom window.

There were two beds, he knew, the larger of which—Helena Stowe's—would be opposite him half-left. His eyes were becoming accustomed to the darkness now, and he could descry a paler darkness there—sheet or blanket—where the noise of breathing came from. The next moment the curtain blew in the wind, admitting a thin diffusion of moonlight, and Stuart Hammer was able to make out on the pillow a woman's head, a body humping the bedclothes, naked shoulders showing above them. All present and correct, he said to himself—and then his teeth bared in a snarl, for, stepping soundlessly nearer the bed, he perceived that it was occupied by two people and the other was not Ned Stowe.

Stuart Hammer was the type to whom unexpected obstacles come as a personal affront, and in whom they arouse nevertheless a strong instinctual response swift as the reaction to stimulus of a chemical secretion. What he did now was not the product of thought, for this was a contingency he had never foreseen, but an instantaneous expression of his personality.

He took the blackjack from his overcoat pocket, hooked his left forearm under the man's neck and bare shoulders, yanked him up from the pillow, and struck him a violent but controlled blow across the temple. Knocked cold before he had properly wakened, the man groaned. Stuart yanked down the sheet and blanket, rolled the body onto the floor, seized the pillow on which the man's head had been resting, and thrust it over Helena's face, as, muttering, she came awake.

Holding it there, he scrambled onto the bed. The woman's meager limbs were beginning to thrash and flounder. He knelt on her thighs, pinning them brutally, and with all his weight and strength forced the pillow into her face. His nostrils flared pleasurably as he looked down at the body squirming like a thin silver fish in the moonlight; but he kept glancing, too, at the man on the floor by the bedside: he should be good for ten minutes at least, with the crack Stuart had given him; but one should take no risks. The blackjack was ready to his hand.

Helena's arms were still flailing, her fingers scrabbling at Stuart's coat or wrists, but more and more feebly; and her attempts to scream were suffocated to whimpers by the pillow that was killing her. One desperate convulsion nearly unseated her murderer, and in an access of fury he punched his gloved fist again and again into the defenseless body beneath him.

When he had made sure she was dead, he put the pillow back over her face and turned his attention to the unconscious man on the floor. A weedy type. Bloody silly that sort of beard looked, over a birthday suit. Stuart felt the man's heart. It seemed to be ticking over quite satisfactorily. So he'd wake up presently and find his mistress dead— a damned awkward situation for the blighter, whoever he was. He'd tell the police he'd been knocked out by an assailant whom he'd not had time to see. But what evidence could the bloke offer to support such an unlikely story? A bruise on the head, which he might well have received during the struggle with his victim? Some missing valuables of hers, which he could have taken away himself to substantiate the tale?

But of course, Stuart Hammer now decided, there need be no valuables missing, no signs of entry, no ladder left against the front wall. Why complicate matters for the overworked constabulary?

Breathing evenly again, he switched on his torch and took a good look around the room. He pocketed the blackjack which lay on the bed, and made sure that he had left no other traces of his presence here. The torch beam lighted upon a chair, a dressing table, a chest of drawers. He opened the top left-hand drawer of the latter and, as arranged, put the front-door key under a pile of Ned Stowe's handkerchiefs. This gave him an idea, and his lip curled sardonically.

The bloke had left his clothes, neatly folded, on a chair by the dressing table. Stuart found a handkerchief in the trouser pocket. His torch beam discovered a laundry mark on it. He pushed the handkerchief under the pillow on which the dead woman's head lay; then, his head cocked as if surveying a work of art, he pulled out the handkerchief again and thrust it beneath the tumbled sheet well down toward the bottom of the bed.

The bearded character on the floor was breathing rather stertorously and beginning to twitch. Stuart Hammer perceived it was high time to remove himself from the scene. He gave a last look round, put away his torch, descended the stairs and let himself out by the front door.

There was no one in the lane. He followed his shadow back to the wood where the car awaited him. The rug was still on the hood. The car seemed to have attracted no more attention than its temporary owner. Stuart steered it very slowly down the woodland ride, got out, peered up and down the lane, listened hard, then at last, settling himself behind the wheel again, took a swig of brandy, switched on the headlights, and drove into the lane and away toward Marksfield.

7   *The Bereaved Lecturer*

THE NEXT morning, Ned Stowe came awake
with a start at eight o'clock, hearing a bell ringing. He
had only slept for two hours. After the lecture the usual
"a few friends who so much want to meet you" had been
invited for drinks by his host, and had asked the usual
questions. Ned answered them in a distrait manner at
first, then found himself talking and talking, as if to
drown some noise in his own head. He was a great success, drank too much and smoked too many cigarettes,
his hands shaking as he lit one from another. It was a
telephone bell which, quite irrationally, he was afraid to
hear; and he had lain awake through the small hours,
dreading its ring, unable now to drown it with conversation.

He dreaded it, though he knew that Helena would not
be found till 10 A.M., when their daily woman came in.
No, he thought, it's not dread, it's impatience, I want to
get it over with—that's why I've had a telephone bell on

my brain all night. I want to know for certain, to end this aching suspense.

There was a bang at his bedroom door, which at once flew wide open, crashing against the wall behind. A grubby small girl, six or seven years old, entered with a cup of tea, most of which had slopped into the saucer, and favored him with a long, inimical stare.

"Hallo," he said.

"Frankie told me to bring you this."

"Oh. Thank you."

This child would be Francesca Lane's daughter. The Lanes, his hosts, were a progressive couple; and the children of progressive hosts were, as Ned knew well, one of the chief occupational hazards of lecturing.

"What's your name?" he asked, sipping the lukewarm, stewed tea.

"Queenie."

"That's a nice name."

"It isn't. It stinks. I would like to be called Doris."

"Well, Doris, what time's breakfast?"

"As soon as Frankie can be bothered to get up, fella. Can I come into your bed?"

"No."

"Are you married to a wife?" pursued the small girl, her beady eyes still fastened on Ned.

"Yes, I'm married."

"Is she nice? What's her name?"

"Some people think so," Ned articulated carefully. "Helena."

"Oh. How long have you been married?"

"Years and years."

"Isn't it time you got divorced then?"

"Buzz off, Queenie, I want to get up.'"

"Don't be phony. I know what men look like. Do you think I'd be good at being a television announcer?"

"You'd be terrible."

Undiscouraged, the child padded over to the dressing table and started examining Ned's belongings.

"Why have you only one key on your ring? Peter has hundreds and hundreds and hundreds."

"Your father has more drawers to unlock, I expect."

"Drawers, dirty-drawers, droopy-drawers, dopey-drawers," the child began to chant, executing a *pas seul* in the middle of the room.

"Beat it! Get out, you little horror!" Ned suddenly shouted at her.

"All right, you fool."

"See you at breakfast, Doris."

"You won't. You'll be dead. I put poison in your tea."

Arrived in London, Ned took a taxi to his club, intending to lunch there. But the hall porter gave him a message, asking him to ring Marksfield 230 at once. So this is it, he thought: but why Marksfield?

"Edwin Stowe speaking. I was asked to ring you. Who am I speaking to?"

"Oh yes, sir. If you will hold the line a moment, I will fetch Inspector Bartley."

There was a slight pause before Ned heard the sound of footsteps receding. He should have filled in that pause with an inquiry as to why the police wanted him. He felt danger closing in on him, and it cleared his head.

"This is Detective Inspector Bartley, Hampshire C.I.D.," came a comfortable, solicitous voice. "I am speaking to Mr. Edwin Stowe of the Old Farm, Crump End?"

"Yes. What is it?"

"We have been trying to find you, sir, for several hours. I'm afraid I have some bad news for you, sir. Very bad news. I must ask you to prepare yourself for a—"

"Yes, yes. What *is* it?" Ned had no difficulty in sounding agitated.

"I deeply regret, Mr. Stowe, to have to tell you that it concerns your wife."

"My wife? Is she—has something happened to her? For God's sake, man!—"

"Mrs. Stowe," the voice bumbled on, "died last night. The circumstances—"

"Died? But—but she was quite well when I left her. I simply can't grasp this." Ned's voice shook. "Did she have an accident?"

"If you will make it convenient to call in at this station on your way home, sir, I will give you such information as we have."

"I'll drive down straight away. Detective Inspector Bartley, did you say?"

"That's right, sir."

Speeding out of London, Ned irritably contemplated another mistake he had made. Should he not have asked this Inspector Bartley why it was the *police* who had notified him of Helena's death? Yet he felt braced, clear-headed, stripped for action. No more uncertainty. The thing was done, and he felt curiously free, as if an enormous weight had been lifted off his heart. He began to think about Laura. A new life was opening to him—a real life, not that death-in-life he had been living all these years. He enjoyed this strange euphoria for quite a time before it entered his consciousness that his own part of the pact had yet to be fulfilled.

Inspector Bartley received him in a room which seemed to be all wooden chairs, dark green paint and filing cabinets. A large man, with mild, steady, disillusioned eyes, he gave Ned Stowe a firm handshake and a neutral look.

"This is a very sad business, sir. I hope you will allow me to offer my sympathy."

"Thank you. But I can't understand—how do the police come into this?"

"You must prepare yourself for a grave shock, Mr. Stowe. Your wife was murdered."

"Murdered!" Ned hid his face in his hands, to conceal its lack of any genuine expression of surprise or horror.

"I'm afraid this is a great ordeal for you, sir. If you would rather I deferred my questions till tomorrow, say—"

"No, carry on. I'd rather get it over with." Ned's voice was harsh with complicated emotion. "Where is she?"

"The body has been removed for an autopsy. At present all we know is that the deceased met her death by suffocation at some time during the night or early morning. The body was discovered by a Mrs. Marle when she came in at 10 A.M."

"Our household help."

"Mrs. Marle summoned a doctor and the police by telephone. She told us that you were away in Bristol last night, and gave us the telephone number of your London club in case you might be calling in there on your way home." Inspector Bartley's voice droned on. Tact, or strategy, caused him to lead up to things by easy stages.

"Suffocation, you said? Do you mean smoke or something?"

"There was a pillow over the dead woman's face. And signs of a struggle."

A struggle—oh God, he said he would be quick, would do it mercifully, thought Ned.

"I do not think she could have suffered long, sir." The inspector's low-pitched, respectfully sympathetic tone set up a revulsion in Ned's mind: he was nauseated by the unreality, the hypocrisy of all this.

"Look, Inspector," he jerked out. "I'm grateful to you for trying to break it gently. But I'd better tell you at once that Helena—my wife and I were not a devoted couple. We had become gradually estranged. She was difficult to live with, and I expect I was too. Oh, we rubbed along fairly well most of the time: but I can't pretend that my deepest feelings are involved."

"I understand, sir." The inspector gave Ned a long, measuring look. If he was shocked or puzzled, he showed no signs of it. "Then we'll get down to business."

A stenographer was sent for, and Bartley began asking his routine questions. Mr. Stowe had been in Bristol last night. What time did he arrive there? Where had he stayed? Name, address and telephone number of his hosts? He had gone there to lecture? Was it a long-standing engagement? Which of his friends and neighbors would have known about it?

Under the steady stream of questions, which seemed so formal and irrelevant, Ned grew restive. Had Mrs. Stowe any enemies? Had she an income of her own? Who would inherit? Had she—at this point Inspector Bartley's voice became just perceptibly more weighted—had she any special men friends? Had Mr. Stowe ever suspected his wife of taking lovers?

"Oh no, she wasn't that sort of woman at all. It's quite out of the question."

"I'm afraid, sir, that my information doesn't bear out that view."

"What on earth do you mean?"

"There were indications," the inspector proceeded, with elephantine delicacy, "that intimacy had taken place. And there were marks of violence on the deceased's body."

"Good God!—" Ned was genuinely startled now—"you mean the burglar raped her before he—?"

"Burglar, sir? What makes you say that?"

Ned felt as if the floor had given way beneath him. "Well, I assumed it had been done by—by someone who broke into the house. Damn it all, who else could have done it?" His heart was pounding so hard he thought the inspector must hear it. But Bartley seemed unsuspicious.

"Ah, yes. A very natural assumption, Mr. Stowe. But the facts do not support it. We found the ground-floor windows fastened shut when we began our investigations. The front door has a special anti-burglar lock, which shows no signs of having been tampered with. Mrs. Marle, who has her own key to the back door, told us it was locked when she arrived—"

"But there are the upstairs windows," Ned interrupted in bewilderment.

"We examined them carefully, and the ground beneath them. I can assure you there are no indications whatsoever of illegal entry. Mrs. Stowe's bedroom window was open; but it had not been forced open."

"Well, I simply can't understand it," muttered Ned after a pause. And he could not. The plan had been that

Stuart Hammer should leave marks of breaking in and leave the ladder against the wall. What could have gone wrong?

"And nothing has been taken?" he dully asked.

"Mrs. Marle found no objects missing. But you'll be able to confirm that, sir. How many keys are there to the front door?"

The sudden change of direction very nearly caught Ned on the wrong foot. "Let me see. My wife had one."

"Yes, we found it in her purse."

"And I've got one." Ned took out the key ring from his pocket.

"Just the two of them, sir?" prompted Bartley. Something in his voice put Ned on guard. Stuart Hammer had arranged to leave Ned's spare key in the handkerchief drawer. He'd apparently departed so far from the agreed plan that he might well have failed to do this too. But Ned's whole safety seemed to depend now on the third key being proved innocent.

"There's a spare," he said.

"And where would that be?"

"Well, unless my wife moved it for some reason, it should be in a drawer in our bedroom, under my handkerchiefs."

"Just so, sir. We did find a key there. Would this be the one?" said the inspector, opening a desk drawer.

"Yes, that's it, I think." Ned was irritable with sheer relief. "But surely you tried it in the front-door lock to see?" he added, rather petulantly. The large man behind the desk let this pass.

"You are sure there are only three keys, sir?" he asked.

"Quite sure."

"And all three are accounted for. You see where that leads us? Mrs. Stowe must have admitted the man herself."

"I just don't believe it, Inspector."

Bartley shifted his bulk in the chair, and ran a finger round the inside of his collar—a habit surviving from his years in the uniformed branch. "Now, here's another interesting thing." He held up a rumpled white handkerchief in front of Ned's eyes, like a conjuror. "We found this at the bottom of the bed, near the feet of the deceased. The laundry mark is the same as that on some of the handkerchiefs in your drawer—in fact we found this spare key while verifying that point. Can you account for a handkerchief of yours being in your wife's bed last night?"

"I certainly can't, Inspector."

"You must pardon my next question, sir. You told me you and your wife were not on the best of terms. There are two beds in the room. Have you, er, occupied hers recently? The night before you went to Bristol?"

"No."

"Was the deceased in the habit of borrowing your handkerchiefs?"

"Only when she had a bad cold."

"Which she did not have when you left her yesterday?"

"No."

"So the obvious explanation for the presence of this handkerchief in her bed is that Mrs. Stowe had lent it to a visitor last night—a visitor who was her lover, and who did her to death."

"It's not in the least obvious—not if you knew Helena.

I tell you, she wasn't the kind of woman who takes lovers. The idea's preposterous. Anyway, if she had a man in there, surely you'd find fingerprints?''

"We have found them, sir. Four sets. Mrs. Marle's and Mrs. Stowe's have already been identified. One of the other two sets will be yours—you'd have no objection to my taking your prints presently, for elimination?''

"None at all.''

"So that leaves the fourth set. They will be the murderer's.''

"What proof have you of that? The murderer might have been wearing gloves.''

"I see you're harking back to your notion about a burglar breaking in. We found clear examples of the fourth set on three surfaces which Mrs. Marle swears she dusted and polished yesterday afternoon. This proves that the deceased had a visitor in her bedroom after four P.M.''

"Yes, but I don't see that it proves anything else.''

"Not proves, perhaps; but it's an indication. Your wife would not be in the habit of taking ordinary visitors, particularly men, up to her bedroom?''

"Well, no.''

"And if a stranger arrived at the door, when she was alone in the house, she'd not be likely to admit him?''

"I agree.''

"You see what I'm driving at, Mr. Stowe? Medical evidence shows that the deceased entertained a lover last night, and that she was murdered by suffocation. All the evidence we have so far shows that the murderer could not have been either a criminal who intended robbery or a chance stranger. So we have good reason to believe that the murder was done by this lover, and to look for him among the circle of your friends and acquaintances at Crump End.''

Laborious though the inspector's reasoning was, and stilted his language, Ned Stowe was impressed against his will by these arguments. That he and Bartley should be discussing Helena's death so dispassionately seemed just another part of the vivid hallucination in which he had been living for many days now.

His line with Bartley must be to remain incredulous that Helena should have voluntarily received a lover last night, or that this man could be one of their friends. It was not a difficult line to take, for Ned felt convinced now that Stuart Hammer had raped Helena before killing her. It was Stuart who must have left those fingerprints, after he had finished with her, while looking round for some valuables to steal, in accordance with their plan. But why had he not gone through with it? Did his nerve suddenly break, alone in that room with the dead woman? What other explanation could there be? Yet Stuart Hammer had not appeared to be a man whose nerve was breakable.

These thoughts raced through Ned's mind while the inspector, who had been called out of the room, was away. He returned now, solid and reassuring.

''That was a call to Bristol, sir. We have full corroboration of your statement about your movements last night.''

''One suspect eliminated, eh?'' Ned could have bitten off his tongue for saying this. Cheap, false and unfeeling. He despised the thing in himself that was always playing up to people. Inspector Bartley's expression did not change.

"Was it generally known in the village that you would be at Bristol last night, Mr. Stowe?"

"I don't know how much I'm gossiped about. Mrs. Marle knew, of course. And some neighbors who came in for drinks a few days ago—the Avenings, Colonel Gracely, Mrs. Holmes and her son, Josephine Weare. A harmless lot."

"Your work entails being in London a good deal, sir?"

"Off and on. But look here, Inspector, you know what villages are like. If my wife had a lover coming to the house while I was away, it'd be all over the village in a week."

"Just so, sir." Inspector Bartley looked noncommittal. But he had, in fact, had a talk with P. C. Rainbird, who like all good village policemen was a filing cabinet of local gossip, and discovered that no breath of scandal had touched the late Helena Stowe. She was considered stand-offish by some, "a real lady" by others, while a third faction felt her as a romantic mystery.

It worried the inspector a good deal that Mrs. Stowe's reputation should be so untarnished. Apart from gossip, a preliminary search at the Old Farm had turned up no incriminating documents whatsoever. Either she and her lover had been remarkably skillful in covering their tracks, or the liaison had only just started.

"One last question, sir, for the time being. And I hope you won't take offense at it. What was your wife's demeanor before you went away this time? Did you notice any alteration? What you might call secretiveness? or suppressed excitement? or guilt?"

"Well, we had a blinding row on Sunday night—she was terribly neurotic, poor woman. But why do you ask?"

"It is possible that she was about to take a lover *for the first time.*"

"Well, I suppose anything is possible. But you don't kill a woman the first time you go to bed with her. You do it when you're sick to death of her, or when she's driven you crazy with jealousy—something like that."

Inspector Bartley made no reply to this argument, which indeed nonplussed him. "You haven't answered my question, sir," he stated mildly.

"The answer is, no. She seemed quite normal, for her, when I left."

But of course this was not true. Ned said it because he had no desire to involve anyone else—to involve them further, at any rate, than they were already involved.

As he drove out of Marksfield, memories flooded back: the sly look, the faraway look, the complacent look he had caught in Helena's eye: Brian Holmes's outburst at the party and Helena's telling him she had played the piano for Brian when he was away. Her air of suppressed excitement at breakfast yesterday. Her unusual solicitude for his health—awkward for her if he'd had to cancel the lecture.

Brian Holmes. A soppy, nondescript young man, about whom he knew almost nothing; but admirably placed, his bungalow and market garden being only a hundred yards or so away, for conducting a liaison with the mistress of Old Farm.

What had he just said to Inspector Bartley?—you don't kill a woman the first time you go to bed with her. No? A young, idealistic, ill-balanced chap might kill a tart, the first time, out of disgust or shame or horror. But Helena wasn't a tart. No, but she was neurotic, one couldn't predict her behavior, she might well have said things, done things, which set up a violent revulsion in the virginal young Brian. He might not have intended to kill her at all—only to stop her tongue with that pillow, stop the endless maddening babble of talk which flowed from it when she got into a hysterical state.

Ned turned off the main road. Where the woodland drive joined the lane, he stopped his car and got out. Yes, there were tire marks here and there up the drive. Picnic parties sometimes left their cars in it. The tracks didn't have to be Stuart Hammer's: but they probably were. Suddenly, Ned saw why Stuart had not adhered to their plan—saw the solution of the whole mystery. Stuart had gone to the Old Farm last night, let himself in, climbed the stairs, opened the bedroom door, and found that the job had already been done for him. He had found Helena dead. Her lover and murderer was already gone. There was no point in Stuart's faking a burglary now: there was nothing for him to do except put the key in the handkerchief drawer. Must have given him a considerable shock, thought Ned. He probably assumes that I went round the bend and killed her myself.

These speculations were swirled away, as Ned drove on, by a flood of relief. Helena's death need never be on his conscience now. He was not a murderer, even by proxy. Fate had intervened at the very last moment, taking the deed out of Stuart's hands and putting it into the hands of Brian Holmes.

8   *The Faithful Dog*

IT WAS the emptiness of the house that, during the next few days, Ned found most insupportable. Yet in a way the place had never been so crowded. When he arrived, there were newspapermen awaiting him. After putting his car away, he let them question him in the yard between the outbuildings and the house; he had nothing to tell them, but he did not try to shorten the interview —anything that postponed his entering the house was welcome. He made a good impression upon them.

A uniformed policeman at the front door saluted him respectfully. Mrs. Marle, red-eyed, dramatizing the part she had been given in the tragedy, emerged from the kitchen and almost fell into his arms.

"I done everything I could, sir," she kept repeating, between sobs and sniffles. She had made up a bed for him in the spare room; the police wouldn't let anyone into the bedroom where poor Mrs. Stowe had been—said they were looking for a weapon or something. Mrs. Marle's wits must be wandering, he thought; Helena had been killed with a pillow. It was not till the next day that he understood. There were telephone messages on the block—inquiries from neighbors, said Mrs. Marle; she hoped she'd done right to tell them Mr. Stowe was expected home this evening. She had left him some supper in the kitchen, to warm up. She really must be off now —didn't know what her hubby would say. But she showed no signs of leaving. Ned had to listen to her account of finding Mrs. Stowe's body—they had wandered into the kitchen now—and reassure her ten times over that she had indeed done everything she could, before he finally managed to get rid of her.

The back door had hardly closed on Mrs. Marle when footsteps were heard clattering down the stairs. A plain-clothes man, a brisk sergeant from the Marksfield C.I.D. branch, introduced himself to Ned, who submitted once again to official condolence.

"I'm afraid I have instructions to seal your bedroom for the time being, sir," the sergeant then said. "I thought you would wish to move some clothing out first. Anything you need for the next day or two."

Ned followed him dumbly upstairs. The bedroom was looking tidier than usual: an impersonal, empty room, the spirit fled. Another plain-clothes man was standing by the larger bed, which had been stripped: he helped Ned to carry a tweed suit, hairbrushes, pajamas, socks, handkerchiefs, shoes into the spare room down the passage.

The telephone rang. Ned hurried downstairs, but the sergeant was before him.

"For you, sir. Someone from the Manor."

"Oh God, why can't they leave me alone. . . . Yes, who is it? Ned Stowe here."

"Bob Avening speaking. Forgive me, my dear boy, I

don't want to intrude on you. My deepest sympathy. It's a shocking business. Don't like the idea of you brooding there all alone. Would you do us the kindness of letting us put you up for a few nights?"

Ned was touched by the little man's diffident courtesy. He was touched; but he realized, with horror, that he must now go through a hell of false pretenses. He declined Sir Robert's offer, but accepted an invitation to lunch the next day.

After eating his supper, Ned wandered restlessly about the living room. He sat down to write to Laura—some cautious instinct prevented him from ringing her up.

Laura darling, he began, *the most terrible thing has happened*—and found he could write no more. False pretenses with Laura, hypocrisy—no, he could not do it: not yet. He had intended that Helena should be killed: she had been killed by another human instrument, certainly; but still, the intention had been there. A violent craving for Laura came over him as he looked at her name on the sheet before him—a craving to bury himself and his guilt in her. He sank to his knees, laying his head on the seat of an armchair, as if on a woman's lap. It was the chair Helena had always sat in: he thought it was Laura's lap, till he heard his own voice muttering. "Forgive me, forgive me."

For two hours that night he wandered about the empty house, feeling as if it were he, not Helena, who was haunting it, bodiless and ineffectual. Once he had been reunited with Laura, things would become real again, solid. But he could not go to her yet: the police would become suspicious if he shot off to live with another woman the moment his wife—No, that was nonsense: the police had the best reasons in the world for not suspecting him, now or ever. I managed that interview with Inspector Bartley pretty well, he thought. But the thought gave him no pleasure, eager though he usually was for self-congratulation.

Next morning he awoke with Helena's voice sounding in his ears. It came from the lawn, below the spare-room window. "Ned! Quick! the daffodils are showing!" He sat up in bed. The mist in his mind cleared. It was not her voice but a memory of it. When they first moved to the country, Helena had taken up gardening in an erratic, unhopeful way, buying a sackful of bulbs and planting them all over the lawn, for instance. Her maladroitness had ceased to be a joke with them by then. "I don't expect they'll grow," she had said, self-pityingly. "Did you put them in the right way up?" "I don't know. Anyway, I've probably got whatever's the opposite of green fingers." But the daffodils did come up. One morning in early spring she called him to look at the first green shoots. He was in low spirits that morning, after one of those degrading nocturnal scenes with her. He put his head out of the window: "Nature's tough—she can even survive your treatment." He did not mean it unkindly; but he saw the radiance go out of Helena's uplifted face. They must have been a symbol to her, those daffodils— if they grow, he and I will be able to start a new life. But he had rejected it. She never touched the garden again.

Funny remembering that now, he thought, trying to stifle the ache of compunction which the memory started. Why in hell's name did she have to take everything so much to heart? God knows I was patient enough, building her up inch by inch—and then one word of mine a little out of place and the whole thing came tumbling down and all was to do over again.

However, Ned had little time to brood that morning. There were a consultation with Mrs. Marle, more telephone inquiries, letters to be written to Helena's parents and her solicitors, his own correspondence to be dealt with—the morning's post had brought two offers of television productions. He was deep in these chores when Josephine Weare turned up.

"Poor Ned, I *am* sorry. Throw me out if I'm a nuisance. But if there's anything I can do—help you with your letters, or shopping?"

"It's awfully good of you, Josephine. But I can manage. I wouldn't think of letting you interrupt your own work—"

"Oh, don't worry about that. Women novelists jump at any excuse for not writing—particularly if it's a chance to interfere in other people's lives."

Her huge blue eyes were fastened upon him with an expression of—was it commiseration or curiosity?—he did not know. It was good to have her company, anyway: her astringent tongue braced him, and she was a relief after the first-mourner presence of Mrs. Marle. Ned dictated a few letters to her; they made a list of household necessities she could buy for him in Marksfield this afternoon—Helena's housekeeping had always been a hand-to-mouth affair, and there were plenty of gaps to be filled.

It was only when she was leaving that Josephine Weare touched upon the disaster. Looking up at him, she suddenly remarked in her light, quick voice:

"You mustn't feel guilty about this, Ned."

"Guilty?" His heart lurched sluggishly, like a waterlogged vessel in heavy seas.

"Yes. I know you and Helena didn't hit it off. Don't

feel you were responsible for that, and for what has happened. I don't expect you could have done any more for her; but, even if you could, there's no use brooding about it now. Think of it as a happy release"—her mouth quivered over the cliché—"a happy release for you both. A release, anyway."

Josephine Weare patted the back of his hand and marched briskly down the path to the wicket gate.

Extraordinary little creature, thought Ned, as he put on a black tie to satisfy Lady Avening's sense of the conventions. A happy release! He *was* aware of some relief, though. It was not Stuart Hammer who had killed Helena: therefore the contract was cancelled—he himself would not have to go through with the Herbert Beverley clause.

Ned's relief was short-lived. He had shut out of his mind the idea of what was to take place at Norringham; or the shadow of the nearer event had blocked it out. But now that event had occurred, bringing the future close with a nightmare rush. Stuart Hammer held his letter to Laura and, unless Ned was utterly mistaken about his accomplice's character, would post that letter to Laura if Herbert Beverley were not put out of the way. Stuart Hammer was a ruthless and unscrupulous man: it had not been necessary for him to carry out his part of the pact, but no such consideration would induce him to give back to Ned the trump card which he held.

Occupied with these thoughts, Ned walked through the village unaware of the glances thrown at him, some hostile, some pitying, all curious. Crump End was already divided into two camps, one of which, in spite of the village constable's assurance that Mr. Stowe had been in Bristol when his wife was murdered, firmly believed that he had murdered her. In a couple of hours' time everyone in the village would know that he had lunched at the Manor. For one faction this would set the seal upon his innocence: for the other, it would prove once again that the gentry stand together in a crisis and cover up one another's sins.

Sipping sherry in the Avenings' library, Ned endured the condolences of his hostess, while Sir Robert sat silent.

"First your poor wife, and then that young Mr. Holmes," the lady concluded. "Well, I always say it never rains but it pours."

"My dear," put in Sir Robert with surprising asperity, "sometimes you are the soul of tactlessness. Do think before you speak?"

"Well, what have I said wrong?" she inquired, flushing.

"Holmes? What's happened to him?"

"He has been taken to hospital, Mr. Stowe. It seems he was attacked on the same night that—"

"My dear girl," interrupted her husband, "you're just repeating gossip. There's no evidence that he was attacked." Sir Robert turned to Ned. "His mother found him yesterday morning in one of their outbuildings, unconscious. He was put to bed at once. Shock and exposure. When he didn't recover consciousness after some ten hours, Ainsley thought it was best to put him in Marksfield Hospital, where they can keep him under observation."

"Inspector Bartley didn't tell me anything about this."

"The young man had been bludgeoned," said Lady Avening.

"That is a possibility, my dear, not a certainty. He could have hit his head against a container of kerosene in the outbuilding—fallen against it and knocked himself out."

"Are you suggesting he was intoxicated, Bob?"

"I'm not suggesting anything. All we know for certain is that he's in a coma and threatened with pneumonia."

"I never approved of that young man, what little I saw of him. I suspect him of leftist inclinations," pronounced Lady Avening. "I should not be surprised to hear that he was an intellectual."

"I trust, my dear, you did not carry your disapproval to the extent of clubbing him over the head." Sir Robert's elfish face remained quite solemn.

"Really, Bob! You do get the most extraordinary notions. And now tell me, Mr. Stowe, what arrangements are being made for the funeral. I would strongly recommend—"

"My wife was a Catholic, Lady Avening."

"Indeed? A *Roman* Catholic?" Her tone suggested that this denomination was as undesirable as leftism. Fortunately lunch was announced at this moment, and Ned was spared further embarrassment. Sir Robert, who was clearly master in his own house, whatever he might appear outside it, kept his formidable consort on a very short rope during the meal, and Ned found himself warming to the little man's tactful charm and the occasional gnomelike twinkle of his eye. How on earth could he support life with such a humorless, stupid, self-important woman?

Such speculations faded, though, beside the mystery of Brian Holmes. Looking back over his last few days with Helena, Ned was increasingly convinced that, in spite of all his preconceptions about her, Brian must have been her lover. But how had he come by his injury? The police were looking for a weapon, Mrs. Marle had told him. If this was true, it could only mean that Helena had defended herself against young Holmes when he became violent. She must have struck him and he had succumbed to delayed shock after getting home.

It was a comforting idea, so far as it went, but it did not survive a conversation with Colonel Gracely that same evening. The colonel had invited Ned for a drink in his comely Queen Anne house on the village green. Sitting in the study, which was lined with cabinets containing entomological specimens and decorated with flocks of exotic stuffed birds, Ned watched the colonel mix him a stiff whisky. He seemed to be seeing these neighbors for the first time. For years the Avenings, Gracely, Josephine Weare had been no more than pleasant acquaintances: neither he nor Helena had formed any close friendships in the village. But now, as though Helena's death had removed a barrier between him and them, Ned was beginning to make real contact with them. Their concern and practical kindness drew from him a response rather like the convalescent's languid gratitude toward nurse and doctor. He was in the limelight now, and the part he was playing suited him. "You can't bear anyone else getting the limelight for a moment," Helena had said during their last quarrel. He had been outraged by the injustice of it then: now, he began to wonder. . . .

"Drink up, my boy. It's a rough time for you. Damnable. I've seen enough sudden death in my time, but I never got used to it. Never. Friends alive one moment, snuffed out the next." The colonel snapped his fingers. "Well, there's no justice. No doubt Bartley'll nail the fella. String him up or put him away for life. Got to be done. Protect society. But don't call it justice."

"I don't. I'm not panting for anyone's blood. It won't bring her back—" Ned broke off, disgusted by the hypocrisy of this. "The fact is, Colonel, I—well, it's an awful thing to say, but Helena and I—"

"Say no more, my boy. I've got eyes in my head. You stuck to her anyway. Stuck it out. So you should—it's in the contract, after all." Gracely's vague gray eyes took on a quick, pointed shrewdness. "You're dazed now, eh? Can't feel the wound yet? You will, though. You put down your anchor in another human being: things go wrong: you want to get away: but when the cable's cut, you're all adrift for a while. Habit, y'know, just habit. I had a mistress myself for several years. Eurasian. Immoral girl. Proper bloody handful. Bored me stiff after a bit, except in bed. But when she did finally bolt, it took all the stuffing out of me: I'd sunk too much emotional capital in her. Drink up."

After a companionable silence Ned was moved to say:

"The police seem to think Helena must have had a lover."

"You don't mind talking about this?"

"No. Not with you."

"Well, between ourselves, it's true. The chief constable's an old friend of mine. Had a chat with him this afternoon. They've identified fingerprints in your wife's bedroom as Brian Holmes's."

"It's incredible," muttered Ned, more to himself than to his companion. "Brian Holmes? Why on earth should she pick on him?"

The colonel's innocent gray eyes regarded Ned calmly. "Oh, not so very strange. For one thing, he's rather like you."

"Like me?" Ned could not keep a note of outrage from his voice. This was the most violent of all the shocks he had recently received.

"Well, like what I imagine you were at his age. Sensitive, a bit priggish, socially awkward, plenty of charm smoldering under the surface. Just the ticket for a woman with a strong maternal instinct."

"Good God!" exclaimed Ned. The idea was so repugnant to him, and its implications so disquieting, that he shied away from it, saying brusquely:

"Do they think he did it, then?"

"They can't be sure, till he's fit to interview. But I'd say not."

"Not?" Ned realized he had been holding his breath.

"No. There's a major snag, you see. They thought at first that young Holmes might have received his injury while struggling with your wife—look here, old son, isn't all this too harrowing for you just yet?"

"No. Carry on."

"Well. Medical opinion now is that the blow he got was so violent it must have knocked him cold instantly—he couldn't have gone on suffocating your poor wife. On the other hand, if he had nearly finished her by then, she wouldn't have had the strength to give him such a blow. And anyway, there was no sign of anything in the room having been used as a weapon."

Ned Stowe buried his face in his hands. It was like a sentence of death. If Brian Holmes could not have done it, Stuart Hammer must have done it. And that left Herbert Beverley to him.

Three hours later, as he sat in his empty house trying
to read, the telephone bell rang.

"Ned Stowe here."

"Ned, it's me."

"Laura!"

"I've just seen about it in the paper. Darling—"

"I started a letter to you, but—"

"Yes. Are you all right?"

He could sense the anxiety behind the detached voice
she always used on the telephone.

"It's been terrible. I was in Bristol when it happened.
It's all a complete mystery."

"Can you speak?"

It was the old formula—her way of asking if there were
others in the room with him. Were the police tapping his
telephone line? It seemed most unlikely, but—

"Well, yes and no," he replied. "Everyone is being
very kind. I shall have to stay here for a week more, I
think."

"And then?" Her whisper felt like an intimate caress.

"Then I'll be coming to London. Permanently, I
hope."

"Yes, Ned. I shall be here."

That was all the conversation they had, but the memory of it carried him through the ordeal of the next few
days—the inquest, the grief of Helena's parents, the funeral, the interviews with solicitors and house agents, the
friendly, nerve-racking talks with Inspector Bartley. Ned
knew he was under no suspicion: his alibi at Bristol had
been carefully checked, and he was able to answer the
police questions without prevarication. He learned from
Colonel Gracely that they were checking the alibis of
everyone in the village for the night when Helena was

murdered, and had widened their search for a weapon with which Brian Holmes had been attacked; but they could do little more until the young man, now critically ill with pneumonia, was fit to be questioned. Ned had received a touching letter of condolence from Mrs. Holmes, and had written back inquiring after her son's health.

As far as Helena was concerned, he had nothing to worry about. But each hour that passed thickened the ice of fear over his heart. Time had never moved so slowly for him, but it did not move half slowly enough. He had nothing in the world now except Laura, and Laura was the whole world to him; and to reach Laura he must go through an ordeal from which his soul shrank.

On a brief visit to London, he found a letter awaiting him at his club. It contained a car key wrapped in a blank sheet of paper. There was to be no reprieve. Three days later, the code message appeared in the Personal column of *The Times.*

And now, on the Saturday evening, Ned found himself sitting in the train to Norringham—he had decided not to take his car—committed to murder, feverishly rehearsing in his mind for the hundredth time all the instructions Stuart Hammer had given him twenty-four days ago. It couldn't go wrong, it couldn't go wrong, it couldn't go wrong, the wheels of the train tapped out. And Herbert Beverley—that domineering, hard-faced, brutal man who had ruined so many lives—what loss would he be to the world?

Ned had chosen a compartment where five people were already sitting, for he wished to avoid any conversation by which he might be remembered. But it was typical of his present state of mind that he had taken few other precautions. The police, he was sure, were not keeping him under observation. He had told Mrs. Marle that he would be staying the weekend at his club, and he had indeed booked a room there. But he made no attempt to conceal the destination of his present journey. Taking a taxi to St. Pancras, a return ticket to Norringham—this was merely giving hostages to fortune. By the time the train reached Norringham, Ned had arrived at that state of trancelike, insentient being, deeper than recklessness or panic, which marks the total surrender to necessity.

The train was punctual, the carefully memorized route to the suburb where Herbert Beverley lived took him only twenty minutes' walking, so he was half an hour early for the appointment. He turned into the cul-de-sac, noted the registration number on the Humber there, walked out into Forest Road again, heard a radio playing a Brandenburg concerto as he passed the gate of Herbert Beverley's house. It was misty out here, the street lamps making aureoles of light in the gloom. Suppose it gets really foggy? suppose the car won't start? suppose the old man decides it's too cold to walk his dog?

Ned forced these thoughts out of his mind, concentrating on the image of a small old man, focused in headlamp beams like a target in the sights of a rifle. He walked briskly on, shivering and sweating in his overcoat, responding to the "good night" of a few hurrying pedestrians. Time and Forest Road seemed to stretch on forever into the blind night. A line of verse repeated itself in his head—*Only an avenue, dark, nameless, without end*—and his blood crawled with dull horror. Turning, he retraced his steps and was back in the cul-de-sac by 10:30. Still quarter of an hour to go. In quarter of an hour I shall have killed a man. *O lente, lente currite.*

He took out the car key, opened the door, quickly bundled himself in. The door closed with a gentle click that sounded like an explosion. The car was facing toward Forest Road. Ned had driven Humbers; he familiarized himself again with pedals and switches, moving the gear lever gently in the dark with his gloved hand.

He had set his watch by the G.P.O. clock on the way from the station. Ten minutes to go. Five. If the engine starts at the first touch of the self-starter, everything will be all right. The engine did start at the first touch. Ned let it run for a minute, then switched on the sidelights and drove cautiously out of the cul-de-sac into Forest Road away from Beverley's house. A hundred yards down the road he turned it, drove halfway back, and stopped in a gap of darkness between lampposts, switching off his lights but not the engine.

It all depended now on Herbert Beverley. Was he such a man of habit that he always took the dog out sharp at 10:45 P.M., always crossed the road at the same place, always walked in the same direction? It was fantastic to rely on that. The whole thing was mad melodrama. Lighted windows glimmered stagily through the mist, between the laurels and monkey puzzles which veiled the houses of Norringham's affluent citizens. A figure materialized on the pavement ahead—a man with a white dog on a lead—outside Herbert Beverley's house.

Ned had the car moving in second gear along the crown of the road as man and dog started crossing it, thirty yards ahead of him now. He switched on the headlights, accelerating violently. The man, blinded by the sudden blaze of light, stopped in the middle of the road, then made as if to move back to the pavement, but the dog was pulling in the opposite direction.

It was all over in a few seconds. Ned hurled the car at the little figure, which stood there stock-still, one hand raised now as if to ward it off. The headlights revealed his face; and whether Ned's nerve broke at the last possible instant, or whether something in that gentle, scholarly face deflected him—a face so utterly at odds with the character of Herbert Beverley as Stuart Hammer had painted it for him—Ned wrenched the wheel over to the left, swinging the heavy car away from his objective.

He felt no bump. He was sure he had not hit the white-faced little man in the black hat and overcoat. But he drove on as fast as if the ghost of a victim were pursuing him, not daring to look round, too terrified to know whether he was unspeakably relieved or unspeakably humiliated by his failure.

A couple of hundred yards down the road he got a grip on his panic and slowed the car to a crawl. And the next thing he knew was a white object throwing itself against the offside window, a furious snarling—Herbert Beverley's bull terrier, the lead still attached to its collar, jumping up at the car, rousing all Forest Road with its hysterical barking, and set to pursue him, if necessary, the length and breadth of Norringham.

9 *The Other Woman*

NED DROVE on as fast as he dared—it would be disastrous to be caught speeding in this car by the police. At the end of Forest Road he was held up by a traffic light, and the dog overtook him. Turning left, he was horrified to find himself in a shopping street, well lighted, with quite a number of people on the pavements staring curiously at the black Humber pursued by the white dog. The street, unless he had lost his bearings altogether, led into the center of Norringham, so he turned left into a wide, boulevardlike road and put on speed, only to be checked by another traffic light and overtaken by the apparently tireless dog, which again started battering itself on the window.

Ned Stowe had never been afraid of dogs. Perhaps this one was playing a familiar game its master had taught it. If so, he could get it into the car and leave it shut up inside; his original plan had been to abandon the car somewhere near Herbert Beverley's house and walk back to the station. It would be worth trying. Pulling into the side of the road, he opened the driver's window, held out his hand to the bull terrier and made friendly noises. The dog leaped again. Its forepaws scrabbled on the top of the door and its teeth fastened in Ned's gloved fingers, biting to the bone.

With the whole weight of the dog hanging from his fingers, the pain was excruciating. He could not extricate his hand, and to pull the dog up into the car would be madness—its intentions were quite clearly not playful. Jammed behind the steering wheel, he had little freedom of movement. He tried opening the door catch with his left hand and bashing the door against the dog hanging outside; but his cramped position prevented him from doing this hard enough to dislodge the brute. Shutting the door again, he put his head out of the window, and struck the dog repeatedly on the nose with his free hand, but his constricted blows had no force in them. He got hold of the dog's lead and pulled upward. This at least took the agonizing strain off his right hand. The animal's body was now held in air more by its collar than by Ned's fingers, and the strain began to choke it, so that presently its jaws relaxed momentarily, allowing Ned to drag his hand out of their grip. He let go of the lead and wound up the window before the dog could recover from its fall and leap through.

The intense pain from his crushed fingers seemed to clear his head. He drove away at a steady pace, thankful that, as far as he knew, no one had witnessed the recent struggle. Looking round from time to time, he saw the bull terrier racing behind him through pools of misty lamplight, bounding along the boulevard like a white fury attached to the car by an invisible bond. His head clearing, Ned realized that he would never shake off the dog as long as he was in a built-up area, with traffic lights and a speed limit. An A.A. sign, picked up by his headlights, indicated that at the next crossroads he could turn left onto the London road. He glanced at the petrol gauge: the tank was full. The rest of the plan had gone wrong, so there was no point in his abandoning the car here. Why not abandon it in London?

He turned left, and soon was accelerating away from the built-up area. Norringham was twenty miles distant before it occurred to him that Herbert Beverley might have recognized the car which had so nearly run him down and reported its loss to the police. But by this time Ned's mind had settled into a mood of desperate recklessness. There was only one thought in it—to get to Laura. His nerve had failed over the attempt on Herbert Beverley: it would not fail again. Everything he had done had been done for Laura, and he was not going to lose the prize now. No doubt, finding his uncle alive tomorrow, Stuart Hammer would post the letter to Laura which Ned had written on the *Avocet*. Stuart was in London tonight, at a reunion dinner of the Coastal Forces: he would presumably return to Norringham tomorrow—Monday at the latest. The letter would reach Laura's flat on Monday or Tuesday. Ned must be there to intercept it.

But what about the duplicate letter? Sooner or later, Stuart Hammer would discover that Ned was living with Laura, and, realizing that the first letter had been intercepted, post the duplicate one. Ned could not spend his life watching Laura's mail. As he drove on through the night, Ned worried at this problem. He could tell Laura that, under the stress of Helena's death, he had written a letter breaking it off with her, and ask her to destroy it unread when it arrived. No, that wouldn't do; the time factor made it senseless. Stuart Hammer had him by the scruff.

And wasn't it much more likely that Stuart would use that damnable letter as a threat rather than a retribution, to force Ned to make a second attempt upon Herbert Beverley? During their talks on the *Avocet,* the two men had worked out a code message to appear in *The Times* should anything go badly wrong—a message fixing a rendezvous (it had been Ned's idea) at the aquarium of the London Zoo. This meeting should only take place in the last resort, if plans failed or some extreme danger threatened. Ned felt there was nothing in the world he feared more than a second meeting with Stuart Hammer: it would be like meeting a figure out of some recurrent dream and finding it was real; or like a man being confronted by the other half of his own split personality.

He had reached the outskirts of London before he realized there was a more immediate problem facing him. How was he to account to Laura for arriving out of the blue, at two-thirty in the morning, with a wounded hand and no luggage? She might be away for the weekend. She might, for that matter, be entertaining another man: why shouldn't she, after all? He had not even written to her during the last ten days and except for one telephone call there had been no contact between them since they parted in Norfolk.

But Ned was at that stage of physical and emotional exhaustion which compels a man to concentrate entirely on the next step and makes everything beyond it seem remote and unimportant. The next step was to leave the car without being observed—somewhere near an all-night taxi rank and as far as possible from

Laura's flat in Chelsea. King's Cross Station. There would surely be taxis there. Ned drove down the Euston Road, and turned right, into one of the Bloomsbury streets. It was still and empty. He got out and walked quickly away, leaving the ignition key in place, the doors unlocked.

He was halfway to King's Cross when his dulled mind at last perceived the danger of what he was doing. A stolen car discovered within quarter of a mile of King's Cross might well cause the police to make inquiries at the terminus; and the driver of a taxi picked up there at 2:30 A.M. would tell them where he had deposited his fare. Congratulating himself on his astuteness, Ned turned away and began walking westward. He was almost dropping with fatigue when—a lifetime later, it seemed—he rang Laura's bell, feeling like a fugitive who has walked a hundred miles to find sanctuary.

After he had rung the bell several times, a window was thrown up and Laura's head appeared. It was typical of her, Ned gratefully thought, that she wasted no time in questions or exclamations of surprise. The moment she recognized who it was in the street below, she withdrew her head; a light went on in the hall, and the front door opened. Ned almost fell into her arms. He had come home.

In the little sitting room, Laura helped him off with his overcoat, poured him a stiff whisky, sat on the arm of his chair while he drank it. Her body was warm and moist from sleep, the coppery hair tumbling over her dressing gown in wild disorder. Ned's grinding fatigue had suddenly changed into a vague, passive, drugged bliss. He and Laura kept smiling incredulously at each other, touching each other, as if to assure themselves that this miraculous event had really happened and they were together again.

"Are you hungry? Can't I make you an omelet, darling?"

"It's all right, love, I had dinner on the train." The moment he had said it, Ned saw his mistake: Laura must never know he had traveled to Norringham. Yet he did not care, he wanted her to know—to know this and everything. If Laura had asked "What train?" he would have told her the whole story of Stuart Hammer, Herbert Beverley and Helena. It was dammed up inside him, clamoring for release. But that strange trait of Laura's which he had always found both sympathetic and provoking—her deep incuriosity—prevented her from asking questions now. She accepted his arrival, unannounced, at this extraordinary hour, with her usual fatalism. Neither of them was to know at this moment how differently events might have turned out if she had said "What train?" and given Ned the cue to unburden his mind.

Laura did not even notice that he was holding his whisky in his left hand. She too was blind with emotion. But presently, when she raised his right hand and kissed it, she saw the wounds, the dried blood.

"Oh, Ned! What have you done to your hand?"

"A dog bit me," he replied light-headedly.

Laura became practical at once, washing the hand, putting on iodine and a bandage.

"Is that better? Does it hurt badly?"

"Nothing hurts now." The quaver he heard in his own voice released a gush of warm self-pity. "Oh, Laura, I've had such an awful time," he said brokenly, and burst into tears.

She held his head close against her, saying nothing,

stroking his hair with little, tentative movements, as though he still were almost a stranger. She was not conscious that this shyness, tentativeness of hers was a legacy from the time when she had been afraid to commit herself absolutely with Ned—afraid lest, if she did so and lost him, she would lose her own self irrevocably.

"Can I stay with you tonight?" he said.

"You can stay here forever, my darling Ned."

"I'm supposed to be at the club. I didn't mean to—I don't know what I've been doing tonight—wandering about—and then the dog bit me, and it was too late to get back into the club—it was locked and I hadn't got a key," he incoherently babbled, feeling a sour taste of shame in his mouth that he should be lying to Laura already.

"It's all right, dear heart. I'm here. Don't worry any more. Don't talk."

Ned was in a daze, like a man who, having lost his memory, finds himself in a vaguely familiar, comforting place. Oh God, he thought, if only I *could* lose my memory.

"You're tired out," said Laura. "Come to bed and I'll put you to sleep."

She helped him undress, and then took off her own clothes. Now they were looking at each other with a different, sightless stare, and Laura gave a shivering cry and they came together like a clap of hands.

When he awoke, the electric clock by the bedside stood at midday. He could hear Laura moving about in the kitchenette. He felt languorous, peaceful: the flood had erased, it seemed, all traces of the last ten days. Perhaps it had been a prolonged, dreadfully plausible dream. The throbbing in his right hand dispelled that fancy: yet he still had this strange, new feeling of wholeness.

Laura came in with a tray of coffee, toast and boiled eggs. They were both ravenously hungry. When they had finished eating, and she had removed the tray, Laura came back and stood beside the bed, looking down at him with a brooding expression.

"Still love me?" he asked.

"Yes . . . You're changed."

"Changed?"

"I don't know how to describe it. Different. Harder, somehow. No, not quite that. Clearer round the edges."

"Well, quite a lot has happened to me since we last met."

"I know, darling. We haven't talked about your wife yet. Would you like to?"

"What is there to say? She's dead. Somebody killed her. The police think it may have been a lover—a young chap she took up with in the village."

"Poor Helena. And you never suspected—?"

"If I'd known she had a lover, do you suppose I'd—?" Ned broke off abruptly, horrified to realize how near he'd come to blurting out the truth. He began again— "do you suppose I'd ever have let you make the break?"

Laura's lip trembled for an instant, but she continued to regard him musingly. "I wish it hadn't happened this way," she said.

"Well, for God's sake! I didn't jump for joy myself," he bitterly replied.

"I'm afraid, Ned." She was very much in earnest, her eyes averted from him now. "It's a bad beginning for us —no, don't be angry with me! I'm afraid of the effect she might have on us—dying that way."

"Oh nonsense! Scared of ghosts?"

"It's your sense of guilt I'm worried about," she patiently explained. "I'm afraid you'll start feeling you were really responsible for it, could have prevented it—if you'd been nicer to her, she wouldn't have taken a lover; and if she hadn't taken a lover—"

"You leave my sense of guilt alone! I can look after it myself."

"All right. But I do feel guilty too."

"Oh really, Laura!"

"Yes. You see—" her voice went into a whisper—"I often wished her dead. I almost prayed for it, lately."

Ned was deeply moved by this confession, for it revealed how much Laura had continued to love him during the time when they had been parted and he had imagined her starting an affair with someone else. He said, tenderly now, "And don't you think I wished her dead too? Often and often?"

For the second time he found himself on the very brink of confession, wanting to pour it all out and leave no vestige of falsehood between them.

"What would you say if I told you that I really was responsible for Helena's death?"

"But you were in Bristol." Her eyes looked uneasy, almost panicky. "Weren't you?"

"Yes, I was. But would you still love me, supposing I told you I'd—well, encouraged another man to kill her?" he tensely asked.

"Ned, please stop! It's unbearable. I don't like that sort of joke. It's not worthy of you."

"I'm perfectly serious. Would you still marry me, if—"

"No, I won't have it. Why are you going on like this? Hateful, melodramatic stuff—it's not like you, Ned."

"So you know exactly what I am like?"

"I know you wouldn't do anything so—so vile and appalling."

"Not even for you?"

She tossed her head angrily, thinking that he was teasing her, testing her—she did not know what, but it was unspeakably distasteful. She turned to go out, but he seized her wrist with his left hand.

"Let me go, Ned. You're being horrid."

He had failed again to tell her. He had given her a chance to hear the truth, and she had rejected it. His sense of moral failure set up an obscure, scorching resentment.

"Come to bed again."

"No. Please, Ned. Don't—"

He dragged her down beside him. Mastering her, he felt as if he were subduing something in himself—something which tried and condemned him. Looking down at her beautiful mouth distorted by pleasure, the head weaving from side to side, the suddenly frantic eyes, he saw for a moment not Laura's face beneath him but Helena's as it might have been when the pillow was stopping her breath; and the voice he had tried to stifle was saying, "Now you *are* damned, now you are damned eternally."

After a long time, Laura whispered, "I love you, love you, love you. . . . You were only joking, Ned, weren't you?"

"Only joking," he replied thinly.

When he rang up his club, to explain that he had stayed the night with friends and would be coming in this afternoon to pick up his bag and pay for the room he had not used, he was told there was a message from Inspector

Bartley asking him to telephone. Irrational fear seized him. Somehow the police must have got on to the journey he had made last night: in spite of his alibi for Helena's murder, he was being followed. Well, he'd soon know. He got through to Marksfield.

"I'm sorry to trouble you, sir," came Bartley's slow, reassuring voice. "I tried to get you at your club last night, but—"

"Yes, I met some friends and they put me up."

"We're still puzzled about the front-door key," the inspector explained. "The spare one we found in your chest of drawers—did you normally keep it on your key ring, sir?"

When in doubt, tell the truth. "Yes, normally."

"Was there any particular reason why you left it behind when you went to Bristol?"

"Not that I remember."

"Your wife hadn't temporarily mislaid hers?"

"No."

"I see. Can you remember missing any of the three keys, or lending one to anybody, during recent months?"

"I'm sure I didn't. Of course, my wife may have lent hers—I wouldn't know. But there's never been one missing."

"Well, sir, I am much obliged to you. You will be staying several days in London? At your club?"

"No, with a friend." Ned gave the inspector Laura's address and telephone number. "May I know why you're asking about the keys again?"

There was a slight pause before Bartley replied. "If Mrs. Stowe did not admit the murderer herself, he must somehow have got possession temporarily of a front-door key and had a copy made."

A minute later, when Laura came in from making the bed, she found Ned sitting by the telephone looking thoughtful.

"Who was that?"

"The police. Inspector Bartley."

"Oh."

Ned was thankful now for Laura's lack of curiosity. He felt considerably shaken. Though the inspector had sounded quite unsuspicious, Ned realized he had made a gaffe by telling Bartley that he normally kept the spare key on his ring. It had not been on the ring for a fortnight prior to Helena's death, because he had lent it to Stuart Hammer. And, since he kept no other keys on the ring, the absence of one might have been noticed by Mrs. Marle—by anyone: that appalling child at Bristol had commented on his paucity of keys.

When he had got back from his club, Ned went for a walk with Laura along the Thames. She clung to his arm, in a dependence she had never shown before. The sun was sparkling on the river: an eight rowed past like a clockwork water beetle, a yellowish-white smoke bellied out sluggishly from the chimneys of Lots Road power station. It was the first time that Ned and Laura had been able to walk together without his glancing involuntarily around him, worried lest they should be spotted by acquaintances.

"We only need a pram," he said, "to be a standard young married couple."

"Not standard, I think. But I'd like the pram part of it." She squeezed his right hand, and he winced.

"Oh, darling, I forgot. Sorry. But oughtn't you to show it to a doctor?"

"I will tomorrow, if it goes on throbbing." Ned halted, and they leaned on the embankment wall, gazing at the river. "I wish I could remember exactly what did happen last night. I suppose it must have been delayed reaction. I went out before dinner, with the general idea of getting tight. Then—I don't know how much later it was—I saw a bloke in the street thrashing a dog. I told him to lay off it. He went for me, and I knocked him down. Then his bloody dog attacked me: a white bull terrier. And after that I must have had some sort of blackout. The next thing I remember is ringing your doorbell." Ned was staring at the river while he said all this, as if he were repeating a lesson to it.

"Poor love. Why didn't you come straight to me?"

"My conventional upbringing, I suppose. Nasty streak of respectability. Simply not done to gallop off to another woman when one's wife is hardly cold in the grave."

Ned was startled by the bitterness with which this came out. Laura was looking distressed. A month ago, he would have hastened to apologize for such a remark, seeking to re-establish himself with her. But his heart felt harder today: he had less compunction about hurting her, now that he was sure of her.

"The point is this, Laura. I'm so vague about last night I don't even know if anyone saw this set-to I had. But I suppose it's just possible the police might start inquiring about it. So, if you should be asked, will you tell them I was with you the whole evening."

"Well, all right, if you want me to. But—"

"I just don't want to be involved in anything else for a while. I couldn't stand it." His voice rose to a higher pitch, almost out of control.

"I'll do whatever you say," she agreed meekly.

And if she can swallow that story about the dog, she can swallow anything, Ned thought, with a flick of cynical contempt for which he was at once ashamed.

The next morning, as soon as the alarm clock woke them, Ned went downstairs and fetched the letters from Laura's box. The envelope he had expected, addressed in his own handwriting, was not among them. Laura left for work at nine o'clock. Ned read the paper, mooched about the little flat, unable to set his mind to anything, feeling as if he were in a kind of limbo. Monday passed, and Tuesday, and by the Wednesday-morning post his letter had still not come. What sort of cat-and-mouse game was Stuart Hammer playing?

Ned had arranged to lunch at his club with an I.T.A. producer and discuss a new series of programs over which they would be collaborating. While he was waiting for this man, he opened a *Times* in the reading room, and the first thing that caught his eye was an obituary of Herbert Beverley.

For a moment he was convinced it must be a delusion. The print blurred and flickered before his eyes: then it settled down. The obituary told Ned two things—that Herbert Beverley had died of a heart attack last Saturday night, and that he had been a model employer of labor, a man of liberal views, high cultivation and upright life, esteemed by all. Even allowing for the *de mortuis* decorum proper to an obituary notice, it was clear that Herbert Beverley had been the very opposite of the character whom Stuart Hammer had described. The face of the man he had glimpsed in the glare of the headlights—a face he had shut out of his mind ever since—rose up before Ned Stowe: he had known then, instantaneously, the real Beverley: illumination had made him wrench the Humber away from his victim. But it must have been too late. The shock of his narrow escape from death must have killed Herbert Beverley.

Ned was so distrait during lunch that his companion apologized for having asked him to discuss business so soon after the tragedy.

"Please don't," Ned answered. "I thought it would take my mind off things. You don't happen to know where the nearest public library is, do you?"

"Public library?" His friend looked at him askance. Poor old Ned was in a very peculiar state of mind. "Afraid I've no idea. Why?"

"I want to do some research."

The hall porter did not know, either. He suggested trying the telephone directory: but Ned, saying good-by to his I.T.A. friend, hurried out of the club. A sudden revulsion had seized him—he did not want to know any more, he wanted to dig a hole for himself and disappear from sight. Yet, seeing a policeman standing at the next intersection, Ned walked up to him and inquired for the nearest public library. As he went in the direction indicated, a mad voice started banging through his head— "Murderer asks policeman way." "No," he corrected the voice, "Man asks policeman show him way find out if he's murderer."

Ten minutes later he was turning over a file of the Norringham *Record.* Monday's issue carried a long account of Herbert Beverley's services to the community, and a short one of his demise. He had been found dead in the road outside his house at 10:50 on Saturday evening. For some years the condition of his heart had caused anxiety. Death was due to heart failure. Tuesday's issue made up for the undramatic nature of Monday's. Shorn of its sensational trimmings and clichés, the story was this: The morning after Mr. Beverley's death, his niece discovered that his car, which he kept in a cul-de-sac near the house, was missing. Police inquiries produced a number of eyewitnesses who had seen the car at several points in the neighborhood, shortly after its owner's death, being driven fast and pursued by a dog. The dog, identified as Mr. Beverley's bull terrier, did not return to the house till an hour after its master's body had been discovered. The car, a Humber, was subsequently found abandoned in a street off the Euston Road. The Norringham police were working on a theory that the car had been stolen by criminals, that Mr. Beverley had seen it being driven away when he took out his dog for a walk, had tried to stop it and been struck down by a heart attack in the process (there were no signs of violence on the body): the criminals, finding themselves chased by Mr. Beverley's dog, had abandoned whatever plan they had stolen the car for—some local robbery, perhaps—and driven it back to London.

The paper also carried an interview with Mr. Beverley's nephew and personnel manager, Mr. S. E. Hammer, in which he expressed his deep sorrow at the tragedy which had befallen his uncle, his intention to do all in his power to help the police bring the criminals to book, and his determination to carry on Beverley's great tradition of service to the community, upon which Norringham's prosperity had been founded, along the lines laid down by his uncle. "It will be my responsibility and my privilege," Stuart Hammer was reported as saying, "to ensure, so far as in me lies, that the excellent relations between management and labor which have always been the proud boast of Beverley's shall remain the keystone of our policy. It is what my uncle would most have wished. There could be no finer memorial to this great citizen of Norringham than the continued prosperity of the firm to which he gave the whole of his working life."

10　*The Market Gardener*

When Ned drove down to the country next day, his mind was full of discordant feelings. Fear of discovery was, to his surprise, the least of these. Though he had killed Herbert Beverley as surely as if the car had in fact struck the old man, there could be nothing to connect him with the crime: he had left no fingerprints on the Humber, for he had worn gloves throughout, and it had been too dark and misty for anyone to see the face of the man who was driving it. He felt an increasing resentment and contempt for the man who had tricked him into the deed by so misrepresenting the character of the victim. Stuart Hammer's cynical hypocrisy, in his interview with the Norringham *Record,* sickened Ned. But, for the manner of Helena's death, he hated Stuart —and hated himself still more.

He had told Laura he must return to the Old Farm to wind things up, remove his personal belongings and arrange for the auctioning of the furniture. She did not argue about it; but instinctively she felt, and he knew she felt it, that this was only an excuse. There had been an anxious look on her face when they parted, for all his reassurances that he would soon be back. What he could not tell her was that he must return to the Old Farm to confront and exorcise a ghost. Perhaps she suspected this, though not the reason for his need to do so. At any rate, he knew now that Helena's death had not broken the wretched bond between them: it would shadow his relationship with Laura, falsify it and make it unreal, unless he could somehow in his own mind face up to the full horror of what he had done.

There were moments, indeed, when it seemed that Laura, not Helena, was the ghost. She had been the Promised Land—a dream for which he had sacrificed everything, a place flowing with milk and honey. But now that he was there, it was not so different from any other country. After the first wild excitement of their reunion, the certainty that at last he had come home where he belonged, there had been times during the last few days when she seemed a stranger to him. He could not focus this flesh-and-blood woman with the image of her he had carried about with him so long. In the cramped little room above the river, while Laura was out at work, the aftermath of physical satisfaction had left Ned with a feeling of hollowness, flatness. What am I doing here? he had caught himself wondering. Was it for this I incurred damnation? Perhaps hell is a place where one is condemned to know love as eternally meaningless.

Ned found he had stopped his car in the lane beside the wood. He was nearly home, he thought; and then— so I still call it home. He obscurely felt a need to pause, to rally himself for the interview with dead Helena. But it seemed she had come out to meet him. As he walked slowly up the ride, smelling the mushroomy autumn smells, he suddenly remembered with extraordinary vividness the first time he and Helena had come here. It was soon after their move to Crump End. They were exploring a new country together, feeling as if they themselves were being renewed. They had lit a fire of twigs and leaves in the heart of the wood and eaten their picnic lunch, with the leaves yellowing overhead as they were now. It was a moment of innocence and hope. Helena stretched her hands over the little fire, in a movement that looked like a vow or a blessing. When she glanced up at him, her eyes were wet. He thought they were smarting from the smoke, till she said, "I will try to do better."

Something was released in him by the memory, as it had been by the event. Of course nothing had come of Helena's wish for amendment: but remembering it now, Ned felt a strange melting of the heart and a closeness to her which he had not felt for years.

His reverie was broken by the sound of a horn. Looking toward the lane, he saw a car drawn up behind his—the van which the Holmeses used for bringing their produce to Marksfield. Mrs. Holmes was beckoning to him.

"I thought I recognized your car," she said when he had walked down to her.

"How is Brian?" he asked.

"Better, thank you. He got over the crisis three days ago."

"I'm glad."

Mrs. Holmes, usually so calm, so much in control, looked nervous. Her hair straggled from beneath the felt hat, and she had buttoned her coat unevenly. She was unable to keep her eyes on Ned as she went on in a hurried voice, "I stopped to ask if you would—I'm in great trouble—could I have a talk with you?"

"Well, of course. But—"

"I know it's a most unreasonable—as if you hadn't far worse troubles yourself. But I don't know anyone else who could help me."

"It's about your son?"

"Yes." She gave him a grateful look for helping her out. "I'm at my wit's end, you see. The most dreadful stories are going round the village, about Brian. And our nurserymen have started not turning up—I've been coping with the market garden almost single-handed for two days. Look, I'm on my way to the hospital now. Could you possibly come and have supper with me when I get back?"

Ned agreed to do so. He had a pretty shrewd idea what the trouble was at the Holmeses'. No doubt, too, Mrs. Holmes thought it might be alleviated once the village gossips discovered that he had visited her house in a friendly way. Ned could feel no objection to being exploited by a mother desperately anxious about her son. Besides, he liked Mrs. Holmes; he remembered the sympathy for him in her gray eyes when Helena had been bitchy at the cocktail party.

His first act, on entering his house, was to ring up Robert Avening and explain Mrs. Holmes's predicament. Sir Robert was shocked to hear of it: he promised to say a word at once to her defaulting nurserymen, and if they proved recalcitrant, to lend her one of his own gardeners.

Ned lit the boiler, and a fire in the living room, for Mrs. Marle had not been warned of his return and the house had a stuffy chill on it. He settled down to deal with his accumulated correspondence. It was still only just after midday, and the rest of the day gaped before him like an enormous hole that must somehow, however uselessly, be filled in.

Presently, taking a grip upon himself, Ned went upstairs to the bedroom he and Helena had occupied. The door was no longer sealed. Entering, he threw open a window, then forced himself to look steadily at the bed where she had been murdered. His mind felt quite numb, unresponsive, stripped. Someone—the police, he supposed—had removed pillows and bedclothes: there were only the mattress and the frame of the bed. A thrush sang in the garden, and children's voices floated up from the road beyond. A breeze fluttered the window curtains. Ned became aware that he was trying to re-create the terrible last scene he had had with Helena here on the Sunday night, and that he was unable to do so. Another scene interposed—Helena in bed with pleurisy years ago, docile and pathetic as a sick child, and himself nursing her. Physical illness always smoothed out, as it were, the kinks in her mind, quietening her, making her passive and unexacting: at such times the illusion had been created that there could be a new beginning, a relationship in which he would take the lead and gently dominate her.

Now, as though the recent past had given way beneath him, Ned found himself fallen through into older memories. It was a kind of trap—the last he had expected. The Helena who had so nearly destroyed him, and whose destruction had seemed an act of desperate self-defense, was not here: her place had been taken by a more equivocal, more disturbing figure—an anthology, as he bitterly put it to himself, of the best extracts from Helena. But this figure, or figment, could not be dismissed with a phrase. He could only harden his heart against it. And, as the days passed, he was to learn that his old defenses against the living Helena were of little avail against this more insidious creature.

For the present, however, there was a respite. Looking through papers in his desk, destroying everything he was not going to take away, Ned came upon the manuscript of his unfinished play. He was about to tear this up too when his eye caught a passage of dialogue in the opening scene, and with an extraordinary sense of clairvoyance he instantly perceived how the play had taken a wrong turning there and how it could be put back on the right road. Clearing a space on the desk, he set to work and soon became absorbed in an imagined world. He felt a new clarity, an incredible mastery. After four hours he had entirely rewritten the first act, and knew he could do the rest.

He rose excitedly from his chair, and the next moment realized that he had done so in order to call Helena and show her what he had written. The real world came down on him like a fog. It was nearly 6:30—time to go across to Mrs. Holmes's cottage. He remembered, but without resentment, how Helena had contrived to nag him about the play, to deaden her encouragement with a kind of pervasive skepticism. Poor old girl, he thought, she couldn't help it, she was so miserable at the failure of her own talent.

Walking through the Holmeses' market garden, he noticed that several greenhouses had panes of glass shattered: there was a heap of broken cloches, too, on a rubbish dump. Mrs. Holmes came to the door of Field Cottage—it was, in fact, a jerry-built bungalow—looking distressed.

"They did that this afternoon, while I was away. Children or youths. I know I oughtn't to be so upset, but—"

"It's a damned shame," Ned put in hotly. "I suppose their bloody-minded parents egged them on." For this too I am responsible, he thought.

Mrs. Holmes laid her hand on his for a moment. "There *are* good people. Sir Robert rang up—he's going to help."

"I'm so glad."

"Thank you for telling him. I do appreciate it."

Coals of fire, thought Ned. His cheek began twitching. There was nothing he could say that would not deepen the falsity of it all. In his extreme embarrassment he was unable to feel hers, till over a glass of cheap sherry in the poky little "lounge" she came out with "Brian admired your wife very much," and then, as though realizing she had said too much or too little, "He was with her that night, you know."

She stared into the fire, her head averted, the brown cheek flushed.

Ned swallowed. "Yes, I know," he soothingly answered, feeling an immense and impotent desire to help her out, and at the same time a dread of the complications which lay between them. To gain time, he asked her about her own life. She had been left a widow ten years ago, Mrs. Holmes told him, while Brian was at school. She had a small income, which with the rising cost of living became ever more inadequate to support them. Brian had showed some talent for music; but he developed lung trouble, and the doctor said he should live an open-air life. Gardening had always been a hobby of Mrs. Holmes': Brian was interested in it too: so, after Brian had worked for two years, learning the job, in a friend's market garden, she sank most of her capital into acquiring Field Cottage and its surrounding acres, taking them over as a going concern from a man who had established a good connection in Marksfield and its neighborhood.

Ned saw Mrs. Holmes as a woman whom circumstances had driven off her natural course—a woman meant to be supported and cherished, who had been compelled to take command, take risks, get things done, and in the process had discovered unsuspected powers. Married to a provincial solicitor, she had no doubt followed the usual pattern—bridge, golf, pottering in the garden, membership in a local music or literary society, being "a good wife." But now, transplanted into poorer soil, she had shown a hardiness which might well have surprised the late Mr. Holmes. She was still extremely feminine; but she bore the marks of a strong self-discipline, and it was clear from the way she talked about her son that one purpose of this self-discipline had been to avoid the classical dangers of the widowed-mother-only-son relationship.

"So you see, it's rather worrying," she was saying. "Apart from Brian's trouble, this cloud hanging over our heads is bad for business. You know what a country district is like. One retailer in Marksfield has canceled his orders already."

She said it without querulousness or self-pity, but there was a faint quaver of anxiety in her voice.

"You mustn't worry too much. These things blow over."

"As long as they don't blow *us* over in the process,"

she said, smiling bravely. "Well, I'll go and finish my cooking. Make yourself at home, please. Can you drink beer?"

"Yes, rather. But don't—"

"I'll bring you some now. This sherry *is* rather foul, isn't it?" For a moment Ned saw what she had been twenty years ago—light and loved and easy. It was odd that such a woman could have produced a wet like Brian.

Ned glanced round the cramped, ill-proportioned room, to which Mrs. Holmes had somehow given charm and character. There were touches of color relieving the shabbiness of the furniture, and one or two exquisite pieces—relics of her more prosperous days. The bookshelves on either side of the hideous little fireplace contained reading matter very different from that usually found in bungalows.

"This is what the agent called a 'dinette,'" Mrs. Holmes was presently saying. "The names they think up!"

The meal was simple, but excellently cooked. Helena would have kept on apologizing for it, thought Ned, ashamed of the thought. Mrs. Holmes expected him to enjoy it, and he did. He noticed she was getting through quite a lot of beer.

"I'm trying to get to like the stuff," she said, reading his mind. Then, flushing a little, "I wish it was Hollands, though."

"Hollands?"

"Dutch courage. I need it." The gray eyes regarded him steadily now. "Well, it's an awkward situation, isn't it? You and me."

"You manage to make it not awkward."

"You were her husband. Brian was—was her lover."

She said it with a precarious firmness, forcing herself to state the situation in its ugly, basic terms.

"I didn't—I wasn't on the best of terms with Helena," he replied, unable to meet her eyes.

"I know. I saw that at your party. But she was murdered, and Brian—the police suspect him."

"Still?"

"I'm afraid so. They took a statement from him yesterday; he was well enough."

"But surely—"

"He admits he was—was with your wife that night. It was the first time, he says. He's very young and loyal, you know. Oh dear, I don't know how to put this, without hurting you. He'd never tell the police, but he hinted it to me—they let me see him alone this afternoon—the advances came from your wife. There, I've said it. Can you forgive me?"

"There's nothing to forgive," Ned answered gloomily. "It must have been my fault. I can't understand it." And he still could not. "But I gathered from Colonel Gracely last week that the police hadn't enough evidence. You said your son made a statement. Do you mean—?"

"Oh, not a confession. You see, he honestly doesn't remember anything that happened after—after he went to sleep. That's the dreadful thing."

"The dreadful thing?" Ned echoed dully.

Mrs. Holmes was staring at him, with a wild, horrified look. All the anguish she had been suppressing broke through, making her tone shrill. "Yes. He doesn't know —he's afraid he did kill her and doesn't remember it."

"What? In a brainstorm?"

"Yes." Her voice became almost inaudible as she

drove herself on. "He said, 'Mother, I remember hating her for it—being utterly disgusted—wanting to hit her.'"

"But the blow he received—"

"He doesn't remember. He could have got it falling against the edge of that kerosene container, where we found him." Mrs. Holmes bit her lower lip to steady it. "Even if he's not arrested, he'll have to live the rest of his life under this terrible shadow—not knowing whether he's a murderer, whether he mightn't do it again —never able to trust himself."

Ned had the sensation of standing on a very high dive. Shutting his eyes, he took the plunge, saying in a loud voice he hardly recognized as his own:

"I know Brian didn't do it."

"You *know?*"

There was a quivering silence.

"I mean, I'm absolutely certain he couldn't have. From what you have told me of him." Ned was floundering. He had not jumped off that high dive; he had been pushed—by some force within, which had at once deserted him. He saw Mrs. Holmes's face, irradiated by hope for a moment, settle back into anxiety. Twice with Laura, and now again with Mrs. Holmes, he had refused the moment of truth, betraying his own conscience. Humiliated by his cowardice, he failed to notice the changed, speculative expression on his companion's face.

Well, good God, he was thinking, am I expected to come out with the whole story of Stuart Hammer? Why the hell should I put my head into a noose?

"Let's move back to the other room," said Mrs. Holmes wearily.

When they were sitting on either side of the fire, and he had lit her cigarette, Ned began:

"I wish I could do something. Perhaps your—Brian will remember more details when he gets better."

"In a way, I hope he doesn't."

"But after all—"

"They would be pretty unpleasant to remember."

Ned gave her a startled glance. There was something neutral in her tone and veiled in her eyes now, which he found disquieting.

"Well, of course, if he did kill Helena—"

"I meant, it would be unpleasant for him to remember what happened after your wife had been killed. Can you imagine waking up to find that the woman you have just gone to sleep with has been murdered? It'd be enough to make you doubt your sanity. Not to speak of the mere physical horror of it all."

"Yes indeed," Ned began uncertainly. "But it may not have happened that way. Helena might have been killed after Brian left her. If he doesn't remember anything—"

"He does remember your wife locking the front door when he went in that evening." Mrs. Holmes brushed back the gray hair from her temple. "Nobody could have got into the house without a front-door key, the inspector told me."

"But he might have left it on the latch when he went out—that's what I was suggesting—and someone else came in."

"If your wife was unharmed when he left her, Brian would have come straight home to bed. The only explanation of his wandering into the outbuilding is that he was concussed or else in a state of extreme emotional shock. When he was a child and in disgrace, he used to go and hide in an outbuilding at home." A tear ran down Mrs. Holmes's cheek.

"Look, you mustn't upset yourself any more. I'm sure it will all come right."

She seemed not to hear this. She stared down at her fingers locked firmly in her lap. "You wouldn't go and visit Brian, would you?" she asked, not looking at Ned.

"Yes, of course," he replied uneasily. "But surely he wouldn't want me to—just at present, I mean?"

"It might relieve his mind a little, if he felt you didn't —didn't hold anything against him."

Now what is she up to? thought Ned. There had been something cryptic, equivocal, in her manner these last few minutes. He was conscious, as he had so often been with Helena, of the feminine mind tortuously maneuvering toward some objective, trying out his defenses for the weak spot.

"I don't hold it against him that he was Helena's lover," he said with a touch of aggressiveness.

Mrs. Holmes's gray eyes rested full upon him now, as she said in her pleasant, low voice, "Would you hate Brian if you *knew* he had murdered her?"

Ned felt as if he was frozen to his chair. The question hit him like a paralytic stroke, making it physically impossible to get out a word for ten seconds. At last he managed to speak. "You mean, am I really glad she's dead?"

Still gazing at him, Mrs. Holmes made the slightest inclination of her head.

"It's true I sometimes wished her dead," he said very slowly, more to himself than to his companion. Then, after another pause, "But now it's happened, I'm not—I think I do hate the man who did it."

It sounded like a confession to him, when he had said it, and he was unable to look Mrs. Holmes in the face. There was something too contagious in her directness, her honesty.

"So you'd rather not go and see Brian?" she asked.

Ned knew he was cornered and the knowledge made his voice sound childishly querulous. "But I told you, I'm certain he's innocent."

"What makes you so certain?" she remorselessly pursued.

He shrugged his shoulders, unable to reply. He saw now that when, a few minutes ago, he had exclaimed, "I know Brian didn't do it," Mrs. Holmes's acute feminine instinct had recognized truth in the words: she was convinced he knew the real murderer's identity, and nothing now could shake her off. Like an echo of his thoughts, she began, "I'm his mother. I shall be absolutely ruthless and unscrupulous if necessary, to save Brian from—"

"He's not even been arrested yet."

"—from madness. From living the rest of his life in fear of madness," she flatly stated.

11   *The Secret Drawer*

WHEN NED awoke the next morning, his mind instantly resumed the argument upon which it had fallen asleep. Last night, returning from the Holmeses' bungalow, he had imagined himself making the grand gesture which would lift the cloud from Brian's head. He imagined Mrs. Holmes, a gray-eyed Athene, nodding approval and with a movement of divine magnanimity accepting the reparation he offered. He was afraid of her; it also struck him that there was no one's admiration he desired more than hers.

But this morning it was the practical difficulties of such a quixotic gesture, rather than its nobility, which occupied his mind. Even if there was not a policeman present when he visited Brian, how could he reassure the haunted young man without telling him the whole truth? What conviction would it carry to Brian if he said, "I know you are innocent. Don't worry any more"?

As he shaved and prepared breakfast, Ned found his dilemma generating irrational anger against Stuart Ham-

mer. Stuart had bungled everything—or rather, he had
done it all too efficiently, not leaving behind so much as
a footprint in a garden bed to suggest to the police that
there had been another man at the house that night. The
damnable opportunism with which he had made use of
Brian Holmes's presence—Ned imagined him congratulating himself on his presence of mind, his speed of
reaction, and utterly indifferent to the possibility that he
might have condemned an innocent man to death for the
crime he had committed. Stuart had even remembered to
put the front-door key in the handkerchief drawer,
removing thus the only thread of suspicion which could
lead the police away from Brian Holmes.

Ned's first idea, he remembered, had been that Stuart
Hammer should leave the key in the secret drawer of
Helena's bureau. He could still feel a twinge of shame
when he recalled how he had come to know of its exis-
tence. The bureau, an heirloom left to Helena by her
grandmother, stood in the drawing room. Several years
ago, after one of their terrible scenes, Ned had flung out
of the house; but then, impelled by a mixture of morbid
curiosity and vindictiveness, he had walked round to the
back and peered curiously in at the window of the drawing room where he had just left Helena: he wanted to see
what she looked like, how she behaved, when she believed herself alone after the degrading exhibition they
had made of themselves. He saw her at the bureau, her
back half turned to him. He saw her fingers turn the knob
of a pigeonhole drawer, while with the other hand she
pressed on a boss of the ornamental brasswork. A shallow
drawer slid out from the side of the bureau. Helena's face
was contorted as she took something from the drawer.
She turned a little, and he could see now that her eyes

were shut—clenched shut. For an instant of horror and
hope, Ned thought it must be poison she kept in the
drawer, so blindly desperate was the expression on her
face. Then she moved toward the fireplace, and he could
see that she carried a sheaf of letters. He knew, though
he could not distinguish the handwriting, they must be
letters he had written to her when first they were in love.
He stood petrified outside the window as she tore them
into fragments and threw them in the fire. He could hear
no sound, but the convulsive movements of her breast
told him she was sobbing.

She was always a hoarder, he thought now, trying to
harden himself against the memory. The possessiveness
which made her keep old programs, broken trinkets,
worn-out dresses, was all of a piece with the character
that refused to let go of a marriage which had long ceased
to mean anything but misery for them both. She had the
frenzied grip of the drowning, he thought; and, the next
moment, in a flood of contrition, he saw how it was all
part of her dreadful insecurity—how she had to grip
every straw in reach. He felt this now with his whole
being, like a revelation, though in theory he had known
for years it was true.

Memories began to pour through the breach in his
defenses. . . . A stuffy, sweetish smell. In their bedroom.
Was it three years ago? four? He had traced it to a drawer
in Helena's dressing table, where, hidden away at the
back, as if by a guilty child, he found a cache of rotting
apples, each with a bite taken out of it. Even these she
had not been able to throw away.

Leaving his breakfast unfinished, Ned went into the
drawing room. He had been seized by an inexplicable

impulse to open the secret drawer. Standing at the bureau, he manipulated drawer knob and boss as he had seen Helena doing. In the moment before the secret drawer was released, it flashed across his mind that it was not respect for her privacy but lack of curiosity about her which had kept him from opening it before.

The shallow drawer contained one article—an old-fashioned book with clasp and lock. Ned lifted it out. On its worn green leather spine were embossed in gold the initials of Helena's grandmother. It looked like a diary or commonplace book. The clasp, though flimsy, resisted his effort to open it. He set off to get a cold chisel, but then was diverted by a mysterious compunction about forcing the book open, and started looking for the key. He tried all the other drawers in the bureau, finding an assortment of keys but none which fitted the tiny lock of the book. Perhaps, as it was all so secret, Helena had kept it in her handbag.

Piled on Helena's bed lay the collection of personal belongings which the police had taken away and recently returned. Ned had been putting off a decision as to what he should do with them when he left the Old Farm. One couldn't very well hand them over to the auctioneers. Bury them? Give them to Mrs. Marle? Send them to Helena's parents?

In the handbag he found a minute key which fitted the lock of the leather book. He flipped through the pages: poems, "great thoughts" and such like, in a spidery handwriting, the ink gone brown—Helena's grandmother had copied them out as a young girl, judging by the date inscribed under her name on the first page.

But then, about two-thirds through the book, the spider writing left off and was replaced, after two blank pages, by one he knew well. Helena had been using the book for her own confidences. The first words she had written there went into him like a knife.

N. went off for his holiday today. I could see he was glad to go—to get away from me. He was kind and distrait, his thoughts running ahead of him. He looked through me when he said good-by, as if he was seeing some distant prospect. Another woman? I don't suppose he's faithful to me. Why should he be? —I'm hopeless, I've ruined his life. If I could stop loving him, I would stop tormenting him.

Before Ned could read further, there was a loud knock on the front door. He felt a moment of panic, convinced that the police had somehow ferreted out the secret compact between Stuart Hammer and himself; but, putting his head out of the window, he saw that the caller was only Colonel Gracely. Still holding the leather book, he ran downstairs to let him in.

"On my way to Mrs. Holmes—thought I'd drop in here first and see if you wanted any help. Damned unpleasant business, all this packing up." The colonel glanced round at the furniture in the hall, already ticketed by the auctioneers.

Ned thanked him. Why is he going to see Mrs. Holmes? Had she asked him over, so that she can tell him what I said last night? he wondered, feeling as if a ring were tightening round him. How easily the animal fear of discovery blotted out the more delicate reproaches of conscience!

"I had supper with her last night," he said, grasping

the nettle. "She wants me to visit her son."

"Are you going to?"

"Would the police allow it? What's the position?"

"There'd be no objection, I imagine. They haven't enough evidence yet to charge him. I had another chat with the chief constable yesterday, y'know. Young Holmes seems to have made a favorable impression on Bartley. Didn't tell fibs when he was questioned, anyway. Trouble is, he doesn't remember anything after—" The colonel broke off, embarrassed.

"Do the doctors think he'll recover his memory?"

"Probably, yes. But they can't be sure."

"What makes the police think he's telling the truth?" Ned asked against his will.

"Bartley is sure that it came as a great shock to Holmes when he told the young chap that Mrs. Stowe had died of violence. You can't act that sort of surprise—not so as to take in an experienced C.I.D. officer."

"But if he'd lost his memory—?"

"Ah, that's the rub. Of course, they'll turn on the heat when he's fitter. But Bartley's a decent fella; and besides, he can't get round that knock on the head young Holmes was given. He knows, if it came to trial, the defense would bring medical experts to swear it could not have been self-inflicted and couldn't have been done, under the circumstances, by your poor wife."

"Well then—"

"Mind you, it's possible theoretically for a fellow to knock himself out deliberately. But the nature of Holmes's injury bars that one. A violent blow which didn't break the skin. Must have been given with something in the nature of a blackjack. And the police have found no weapon of that kind here, or at Field Cottage, or in between."

"But in that case what on earth do they—how can they account for it at all?"

"They can't. They're properly up the pole. Y'know how the police hate theorizing without facts. Well, they've been reduced to theorizing over this. Just shows you. Theory number one—burglar got in— either young Holmes was wrong in thinking the front door had been shut, or there was a ground-floor window open which the burglar locked behind him when he entered—and that's unlikely enough for a start. Burglar goes upstairs, enters bedroom: Brian Holmes wakes up and gets clubbed—trying to protect your poor wife, maybe. She starts calling for help, and the chap silences her with a pillow."

"Why not with his blackjack or whatever it was?" asked Ned, after a pause during which he had been forcing himself to digest this so-nearly accurate account of what Stuart Hammer must have done.

"Goodness knows," said the colonel. "Fella might have lost his head."

There was another silence in the sunny drawing room where they were sitting.

"You said, 'theory number one.' Is there another?"

Colonel Gracely's mild eyes wandered uneasily: he looked awkward, almost guilty. "Shouldn't be telling you this, old chap. Indiscreet. But of course it's quite fantastic. Well, here goes. Bartley conceived the idea you might have paid some thug to—lent him a key, and so on and so forth."

"*Paid* someone to murder my wife?" Ned's voice rose

in a tone of what was almost genuinely righteous indignation.

"Now steady on, old son. Of course it's a perfectly crazy notion. Anyone who knows you would know that. But you weren't on good terms with her—and Bartley couldn't find anyone else with any motive— forget it, my dear chap," the colonel hastily added, misinterpreting the consternation on Ned's face. "I happen to know Bartley isn't thinking on those lines any more."

"Well, I couldn't *dis*prove it," Ned remarked, controlling his voice.

"You don't have to," said the colonel, a slight military snap in his tone. "Poor old Bartley's scraping the bottom of the barrel now. For instance, a Marksfield chap ran his car into the ditch, just this side of the town, in the small hours of the night your wife—Chap told his friends next day he'd been nearly run down by a car he tried to stop for help, coming in this direction. Well, it finally gets to Bartley's ears, and he asks the Marksfield chap if he took the number of the car. Chap says he did, tells Bartley the number—and the car turns out to belong to a harmless bloke in Norringham, who was quietly at home all that night. Obviously the Marksfield fella was tight and got the number wrong. Just shows you the sort of blind alleys the police are chasing up."

Ned tried to show only a mild interest in the colonel's anecdote, but his mind was seething. To ask the name of the Norringham man would look decidedly odd. It would be a remarkable coincidence for two men from Norringham to have been in the vicinity at that time. The ruthless motorist must surely have been Stuart Hammer:

yet the police were satisfied the owner of the car had been "quietly at home all that night."

Or so Colonel Gracely said. After his visitor had left, Ned began to wonder if Gracely's indiscretions had not been calculated. Suppose he had been deputed by Bartley or the chief constable to try him out, act as an *agent provocateur,* lay some sort of trap for him? The police had, at any rate, entertained the idea that Helena might have been killed by an accomplice of his. It positively irritated Ned that such a farfetched notion should have entered their heads. But it had; and the colonel might be acting on their behalf, laying seeds of doubt and fear in Ned's mind, so that he should try to get in touch with his accomplice and lead the police to the murderer.

Ned's instinct for self-preservation was now thoroughly roused, and the effect of this was that he saw danger and double-talk everywhere. Perhaps Mrs. Holmes had been tipped off to lead him on, too. Perhaps the police had already sensed a connection between Herbert Beverley's death in Norringham and the presence of a Norringham car near Crump End the night Helena was killed: perhaps they were grilling Laura this very moment about his movements last Saturday evening.

Thank God they had not found Helena's diary— heaven knows how much it might not have strengthened their suspicions. Ned pulled the book out of his pocket, where it had been nudging at him during the colonel's visit. Flinging himself on to a sofa, he opened the book with a heavy sense of fatality, like a huge stone on the stomach, weighing him down, as if not till now had he faced the worst.

It's lonely with N. gone. I don't seem able to settle to anything —yet I ought to be used to it—he's like a visitor in his own house when he is here. I suppose I ought to be doing a thorough clear-out with Mrs. Marle, but what's the use? Seven devils might enter, each worse than the previous resident. I wonder what N. is doing in Norfolk. He never even asks me to go on holidays with him now.

Brian Holmes came in after tea, with a bunch of flowers for me. It's a long time since anyone gave me flowers. I used to dream of huge bouquets, after I'd played the "Emperor" with Toscanini. Bloody fool. I wasn't even good enough for a Saturday afternoon at the Wigmore. The devil always got into my brain and my fingers, like a freezing fog. B. H. asked me to play for him. Astonished myself by doing so. All thumbs of course, but it was like beginning to thaw. He's very young—ten years younger than me at least.

Ned ran his eye rapidly over the next two pages. They offered nothing but brief, factual entries. Then he came to a longer passage:

Heard from N. this morning. He writes like an unwilling child sat down to write a letter when it wants to be out of doors. The pen of an unready writer. Why does he do all this wretched pot-boiling stuff for television, etc.? He had talent once. So had I. We've destroyed each other that way too—no, that's not fair, he did his best for me in the early days at any rate—it was my devil that ruined me.

I smelt the paper to see if there was a woman's scent on it from his fingers. Why should I care? But I do.

He says he is leaving Brackham Staithe and going on a sight-seeing trip, ending up at Yarwich. Ned sight-seeing? —it doesn't sound at all like him. And what is there to see at Yarwich? Oh, what a suspicious, impossible bitch I've become!

Thank God the police didn't find this diary, thought Ned again. They could have traced my movements: the constable I ran into on Yarwich docks would tell his story; they would discover that Stuart Hammer had been sailing *Avocet* on this part of the coast; there'd be inquiries at Yarwich and the Nelson Arms.

But perhaps Bartley *did* find the diary, and replaced it to lull me into a sense of security. Oh, don't be such a bloody fool—the police don't work like conspirators in a corny spy story. Bartley has never questioned me about my holiday, and it's the first thing he'd do if he had any suspicions.

Brian and I played some sonatas this evening. He's not too bad for an amateur—fingering good, but a flautist needs sound lungs—he can't sustain a long run.

I think the last time I was really happy was when I nursed N. through that illness, five years ago. Perhaps I ought to have married a permanent invalid.

Funny how Brian reminds me of N. when I first met him. The same unformed, unpredictable character: prickly, quixotic, loyal: a streak of queer integrity, but no moral stamina (who am I to talk?). I fell in love with him most of all for some restless, reckless quality I sensed beneath the surface. It excited me. I wonder is that true. Perhaps it was the child in him I married: the dear little scruffy lost boy. What a pity he never grew up. He would have, if we'd had children. Probably. And probably I'd have ruined the children's lives, instead of his, with my dreadful insatiable need for love. Or is it power—the need for people to be always responding to me? These terrible scenes N.

and I have: I provoke him beyond endurance, simply to get a response from him—hate, lust, fury, even disgust—I don't seem to mind what it is as long as there is some response. I'm unfit for human—I ought to let myself be put away in a mental home but I am so frightened.

O God, help me.

Ned forced himself to read it through again, wincing, his feelings in confusion. So Brian Holmes was his double, his stand-in. That damp, ineffectual young man. Colonel Gracely too had noticed the resemblance. And Helena, a victim of her psychological pattern, going to bed with his bearded shadow . . .

There was a gap of several days in the diary. Then:

N. returns today. For some reason I dread it—not because of Brian though. It must be the fear of going again into the desert which N. and I create when we are together. Last night I was desperate, and Brian saw it, and I made him kiss me. What a squalid little triumph! I must face this—that for the first time since we married I am contemplating being unfaithful to my husband. Mortal sin. B. is very sweet, but I feel as cold about it as a whore. I can only pray for a miracle to save me.

Helena had written nothing in the book after his return from Norfolk, till the day he went to Bristol. This last entry was in an agitated, jerky handwriting, and the ink had been smudged here and there.

Ned has left, looking ill and exhausted. It is my fault. I feel as if my last chance had gone. What is this devil that possesses

*me and makes me torment the one person in the world I love?
I would rather see disgust or hatred in N's eyes than indifference.
If I killed myself—but that is forbidden—he might remember
only the good things about me: my ghost would be easier for him
to live with than I am. I behave like a bitch and a madwoman,
but I am not vindictive, I am not. The only thing I can do now
for N. is to release him—he wants it, he said so. But I haven't
the strength to let go of him. So I shall take Brian as a lover,
tonight—in misery and despair—plunge into damnation with
my eyes open. I shall tell N. when he comes back: it will cut the
silver cord.*

Here the diary broke off. Perhaps she had heard
Brian Holmes at the door. Rising to his feet, Ned
Stowe stared at himself in the mirror, as if trying to
see the man Helena had seen. The lips of the man
moved. "So she died in vain, after all," he was sardonically, wretchedly saying. She had been going to
give him grounds for divorce. She need not have
been killed, nor Herbert Beverley. He could have
gone to Laura with a clear conscience, and begun a
life with her which would not have been—as now it
was doomed to be—a *ménage à trois.* The eyes of the
man in the mirror seemed to be searching out his se-
crets, sparing him nothing. Yes, he confessed to the
relentless inquisitor, I am dishonest through and
through—I told Laura and Stuart Hammer that I
could not leave Helena because she held the purse
strings: it was a lie, told to cover up an even more
shaming truth—that I lacked the moral courage to
break with her finally. "The silver cord." Yes. "The
dear little scruffy lost boy." Yes—Helena was mother
more than wife to me. I depended upon her, hurt

her, lied to her; and if I had torn myself away from her, I should have left the greater part of myself in her hands.

The curtains puffed in a sudden wind, and somewhere in the house a door banged. Seized by superstitious fear, Ned tore the diary pages out of the book, and running into the kitchen opened the anthracite stove. No, he thought, no—you can't destroy her memory as easily as that: you've got to live with it, so you'd better start now. He folded the diary pages and put them in his wallet, then returning to the bureau replaced the book from which he had torn them in the secret drawer.

The solitude of the house was no longer an absence of company: it had become a positive thing, following him as he roamed restlessly from room to room, inhabiting each room like a solid physical presence, speaking to him through the labeled furniture awaiting the auction—speaking more and more impatiently, as though eager to be rid of him and to occupy the house alone.

A hand-painted bowl on the mantelpiece suddenly recalled to him, with the most intense and detailed vividness, the occasion when he and Helena had bought it: he remembered the cluttered little shop in Marksfield, the proprietor's mustache and watering eyes, the very gesture with which Helena, smiling gleefully at him, had opened her purse. He scraped off the label, and wrapping the bowl in newspaper put it into one of his kit bags. Laura could make what she liked of it. Knowing Laura, he thought, she probably won't make any comment on it at all—she's wonderful at not making scenes, at sparing my feelings; but is she capable of understanding that I don't always want them spared?

He tried to think about Laura, to conjure up naked images of her; but it was too difficult, here and now. Dismissing her from his mind, Ned telephoned to Inspector Bartley and the Marksfield Hospital.

12 *The Aquarium Meeting*

ON SATURDAY afternoon, a week later, Ned
Stowe passed through a turnstile of the zoo and made his
way toward the aquarium. After visiting Brian Holmes in
the hospital, and an interview with Inspector Bartley, he
had sent to *The Times* for insertion in the Personal column the code message which he and Stuart Hammer had
agreed upon, to be used only in extreme emergency,
requesting a rendezvous at the aquarium. Hammer's
code reply, fixing it for the following Saturday, appeared
in the paper two days later. No doubt it had been difficult
for him to get away from the works any sooner; and
besides, their meeting would be less conspicuous in the
weekend crowds here.

As he sat down on a bench, where he could keep the
aquarium entrance in view, Ned looked cautiously
around him. He was fairly sure that he was not under
police observation, but the rendezvous had inevitably
some risk attached to it. After that one devastating question which Bartley had asked him a week ago, Ned could

hardly have retained a complete sense of security.

He had taken a taxi just now from Laura's flat to Paddington Station, where he dived into the Underground and took a Bakerloo train. The long ride from Chelsea to Paddington, and his own long sight as he kept watch through the back window of the cab, assured him there was no vehicle on his trail. But for all that, his heart still felt a load of vague apprehension as he studied the faces in the crowd that sauntered past, enjoying the brisk dry autumn afternoon.

There were ten minutes to go before the time appointed. Relaxing his vigilance, Ned allowed his thoughts to be drawn back to the private room in Marksfield Hospital and the ravaged face of Brian Holmes. Brian was looking ill, defenseless, and for all his beard extremely young—young enough almost, thought Ned, searching the white face on the pillow for the resemblance to himself which others had seen, to be his own son. It roused in him a sudden compunction, akin to tenderness.

"Don't worry," he had said, taking the limp hand, "it's going to be all right."

Brian looked up at him, with the grateful, dull expression of a sick animal. "It's good of you to come."

Ned talked for a little about Brian's mother and the market garden; thanks to Sir Robert's and Colonel Gracely's good offices, everything there was under control again.

"Oh, everyone's been very kind," said Brian, with a faint flick of irony that struck Ned's tender conscience like a rawhide whip.

"I hope the police haven't been badgering you too much," he said.

"It's not the police." The young man's voice was all at once saturated with misery, and the haunted look returned to his eyes. Ned felt that Brian had locked himself up again in his cell of despair—one could only communicate with him through a small grille. "If only I could *remember!*" muttered Brian, his fingers writhing together on the counterpane. "She was so sweet to me. I admired her so much. Until—"

Ned helped him out. "Until she seduced you?"

The young man involuntarily nodded, then gave his companion a horrified look. "To be talking to *you* about it! I must be going mad."

"It may help you to remember."

The firmness in Ned's voice enabled Brian to control himself. "I didn't mean to—when I went there, I was going to have supper and some music. Helena said how lonely she often was. She began to cry. Well, what could I do?" He was talking to himself again; Ned might not have been in the room. "She—I'd never had a woman before—I didn't know—I really did love her, but she made it all so coldblooded, so mechanical: I might have been a dummy—yes, a dummy for an experiment. She was just making use of me." Brian's lusterless eyes brightened for a moment. "Yes, I see now. I was a substitute." He gazed fully at Ned. "For you."

"I expect that was it, Brian," Ned gently put in.

"So after it had happened, I felt—oh, like my gall rising—a sort of slow, furious boiling-up inside me. I wanted to hit her, shake her, make her aware of me somehow—of *me.*"

"But you didn't harm her then?"

"No. I found I couldn't. You see, she began to cry again. Crying and sobbing. It made me feel cold toward

her, though: sort of detached and hopeless. I'd had
enough. I thought perhaps her crying was just another
trick, to excite me again. I couldn't trust her any more.
I'd thought she loved me, you see."

"And then?"

"Well, I must have gone to sleep."

"And then," said Ned strongly, "you were waked up
and somebody hit you."

The spark appeared again in Brian's eyes, and was as
quickly extinguished. "Somebody—? No, it's no good.
I can't remember."

Ned took him by the wrist. They were alone together
in the room. If there was a dictaphone rigged up, or a
policeman with his ear at the keyhole, it could not be
helped. "You didn't do it! I *know* you didn't do it! For
God's sake, get that into your head!"

But it was no use. Brian's head rolled weakly on the
pillow, there was no fight in him. "I shall never know,"
he almost petulantly wailed, tears in his eyes. "They
might as well hang me and have done with it. Oh God,
why did I—? I can't forgive myself."

"It's me you should try to forgive." Ned gazed at him
strangely—his *alter ego,* his substitute, his victim—and
said good-by.

Five minutes later, he was in Bartley's office. A recol-
lection of a Simenon novel, in which the murderer kept
forcing his company upon the detective officer, floated
into Ned's mind. The first time he had sat here he had
congratulated himself on his impunity. Now, like a child
caught pilfering, he imagined the inspector's eyes fixed
upon his right hand—the hand scarred from the bite of
Herbert Beverley's dog—and hid it in his pocket after
Bartley had shaken it.

"I've just been visiting Brian Holmes," he said. "How much longer are you going to keep him in suspense?" Guilt, and something else, sharpened his voice: the question was rapped out in a positively officer-class way.

"It's not in my hands, sir," Bartley replied.

"You mean, you haven't enough evidence?"

"We don't charge a man just for the sake of charging somebody," said Bartley with repressive dignity.

"You can't really believe he did it."

"Oh, what I *believe*—" Bartley broke off, aware of a lapse from official decorum. More to get things back on an impersonal footing than out of curiosity, he went on, "Does the name Arthur Lee mean anything to you, sir?"

"No. Why?"

"Or Stuart Hammer?"

Ned felt a sense of suffocation. It almost startled him that he could, in a moment, breathe and speak. "Stuart Hammer? No."

"To the best of your knowledge Mrs. Stowe was not acquainted with either of these men?"

"No."

Inspector Bartley began to explain about the car with the Norringham registration plate.

"Oh yes. Colonel Gracely mentioned that to me."

"Indeed, sir?" said Bartley, privately registering disapproval of his chief constable's tendency to gossip with the colonel. However, this pleasant Mr. Stowe was the murdered woman's husband: he had a right to know what the police were doing about it—to know that they were not leaving even the unlikeliest stones unturned. Bartley had heard only this morning from the Norringham police, he now told Ned, that the owner of the car, a Mr. Arthur Lee, had after further questioning admitted he'd lent it for a couple of nights to his friend Stuart Hammer. They had, in fact, swapped cars—something to do with a bet.

"And they've interviewed this Stuart Hammer, I suppose?" Ned hoped he sounded interested but not very interested.

"Yes. It seems he has an alibi for the night in question. Not that we really expected anything from this line of investigation."

"An alibi?"

The inspector's large ears turned slightly pink: he had never quite got over a tendency to be shocked at the way certain types of people leaped into bed with one another. "He was sleeping with a maid at the country club where he resides."

"I see." Ned saw nothing, except that Hammer must have bribed the maid heavily to give him this alibi; and a person who can be bribed can also be broken down.

"So that's another dead end, is it?" he asked.

"I'm afraid so, sir. Unless some connection between your wife and Mr. Hammer could have been established."

"Quite so. Which means you're back at Brian Holmes, or some mysterious X?"

The inspector shrugged his massive shoulders.

"You've *got* to find the man, Bartley," Ned urgently pursued.

"I understand your feelings, sir. Naturally, you want your wife's murderer—"

"Oh, it's not retribution I'm after. I'm concerned about the living. Brian Holmes—and his mother."

Ned paused. He was giving Bartley his chance: if Mrs. Holmes had reported to the inspector that "I *know* Brian didn't do it" of his, now was the time for Bartley to bring it up. But all the latter said was:

"I'm afraid there's nothing for it but patience. If Holmes recovers his memory under treatment, he may be able to give us a description of the man who attacked him."

"So you do believe he's innocent."

"Frankly, sir, on our present evidence, yes. You can't get round that blow he received. The doctors are quite firm it couldn't have been self-inflicted. It must have knocked him out instantaneously, which means Mrs. Stowe—"

"Yes, yes, that's understood."

"And no weapon has been found. Oh, it's a proper riddle, sir."

"And if Brian fails to recover his memory, he'll go through life thinking he may be a murderer. . . ."

With those words buzzing in his brain like a vindictive hornet, Ned now saw a stocky, cocky figure—recognizable to him, without the beard and the eyeshade, only by its gait—strolling toward the aquarium entrance. The man might have walked out of a dream or a history book, so remotely unreal did the nature of their original meeting seem now to Ned. He himself might have been a youth waking up from the stupor of intoxication to see on the pillow beside him the raddled, rumpled face of a prostitute who, the night before, had been Aphrodite.

Grimacing sourly, Ned rose to his feet. For a minute he attentively watched the stream of people who were following Stuart Hammer into the aquarium: none of them looked like plain-clothes men—not that he flattered himself he could infallibly recognize the type. Then he joined the stream.

Stuart Hammer, though he anticipated no danger, had taken his own precautions. He did not believe he was under police observation; but Ned wouldn't have stuck that S.O.S. message in the Personal column without some reason.

Standing in front of a tank near the entrance, he watched a large turtle pursue a smaller one, snapping viciously.

"Naughty, naughty!" he said aloud.

"Somebody ought to do something about it," remarked a weedy little man beside him in an adenoidal voice.

"Plunge in and rescue the little flipper, mate, if it worries you," said Stuart.

"You've no call to use that tone to me."

Stuart Hammer was about to take it further when, beyond the aggrieved little man, he saw Ned Stowe, who with the slightest jerk of his head indicated that Stuart should follow him, and made for the exit. Stuart was not best pleased. Clearly the aquarium was too crowded for any private conversation; but Stuart, particularly since Herbert Beverley's death, was accustomed to giving the orders, not taking them. However, he followed Ned Stowe at a distance of thirty yards or so, out of the zoo, until they reached an open, grassy space in Regent's Park. In the middle of this, under a tree, there were two unoccupied green chairs, back to back, one on either side of the slender trunk. Ned sat down. Stuart Hammer took the other chair, lit a cigar, and studied the terrain. Old

Ned—you had to hand it to him—had chosen a good place: nobody could approach without one of them spotting him.

"Well, here we are again. What seems to be the trouble?" he asked carelessly.

"Brian Holmes may be arrested for the murder of my wife."

"Brian Holmes? Never heard of him."

"Don't you read the papers?"

"Only *The Times,* chum. Who is this fellow?"

"He's the fellow you found in bed with my wife and hit over the head."

"Oh, him. Weedy type. Gave me quite a turn, finding him there. You might have warned me."

"Well, what are we going to do about it?"

"Do about it?" said Stuart sharply. "What the hell should we do about it? Damn-all, of course. Have you dragged me up to London just to—?"

"Pipe down. Ticket collector."

As he fumbled for coppers, Stuart reflected that Ned Stowe had got decidedly above himself since their last meeting: or was it that the blighter had lost his nerve? Handing the coins to the ticket collector, Stuart twisted in his chair, trying to get a look at his companion, but only the back of his head was visible.

When the man had moved on, Ned remarked, "What was the idea, knocking Holmes out like that? You might have killed him."

"Sorry. Didn't know at the time he was a friend of yours," Stuart replied with heavy facetiousness. Then his voice hardened. "Should I have waked him up and asked him to watch while I— Don't be such a bloody silly clot."

"And then—" the voice at Stuart's back changed timbre—"and then you had to knock Helena about before you— You seem to have lost your head completely."

Stuart Hammer was in a cold rage now. "*I* lost my head? And what about you, little man? You bungled your job nicely—lost your nerve and couldn't even drive the car straight."

"Well, he's dead, isn't he? What more did you want?"

"No thanks to you. Clear off, sonny!" This last was addressed to a child who had come up and was staring at Stuart Hammer. The child threw a ball in his direction. Hammer picked it up and flung it violently away; the child stumbled after it, howling.

"What particularly sickens me," Ned went on, "is the lies you told me about your uncle. He was obviously worth ten of you. And that nauseating, hypocritical interview you gave the Norringham paper."

Hammer jerked round in his chair, glaring at the back of his companion's head. "A little more of that, and I'll start breaking you up."

"You won't start anything, Hammer. You and I brawling in public might lead the police to suspect there was some connection between us."

Stuart took a grip on himself. He felt baffled, which made him all the more dangerous. Ned Stowe, he sensed, was a different proposition from what he had been on the *Avocet;* if only he could see the fellow's face, he could judge how to deal with him.

"Sorry, old man," he said, after a pause, "but you did rile me, you know. Now, let's get this straight. What exactly is in your mind?"

"We can't let Brian Holmes be hanged."

"But he's not even been arrested yet, has he?"

"Nor can we let him go through the rest of his life believing he's a murderer."

"You've come over bloody moral all of a sudden, haven't you?" said Stuart lightly. "What are we supposed to do about this chum of yours?"

"If he's put on trial, we come clean—written confession. If he's not, but he fails to recover his memory, I shall tell him the whole truth, privately, to set his mind at rest."

Stuart Hammer gasped. "Have you gone off your head? Oh dear me no, sonny. No bid."

"Or I could turn Queen's evidence," came the quiet, strained voice at Stuart's back.

"So you *have* lost your nerve, you—" Stuart powerfully restrained himself. "Now look here, old man, what *is* all this about? We're sitting pretty—"

"Not as pretty as you think."

"Come again?"

"The police are onto that car swap you did with Arthur Lee. They've only to start getting interested in my movements the night Herbert Beverley was killed, and they'll break us wide open."

"Why get windy about it, Ned? I'm not worrying." Stuart told Ned about his alibi. The night he had driven down to Crump End, he had made an assignation with the blonde, Peggy, at 9 P.M. when she came off duty, in his bedroom. He put a strong sleeping powder in her drink, and they went to bed. As soon as she was asleep, he left the country club, unnoticed, by a side door. He had previously parked Arthur Lee's car in a quiet road a few hundred yards from the club, to avoid the risk of being seen taking it out from the club garage. When he got back, soon after six the next morning, Peggy was still asleep in his room. He undressed and got into bed. When he woke her, at seven, so that she could go about her duties, Peggy had no conceivable cause to doubt that he had been sleeping with her all night. It was a nuisance that old Arthur had finally told the police about the swap: but Stuart had originally asked him to keep it quiet so that no gossip about the bet should reach Herbert Beverley's ears: Herbert being dead, Arthur had naturally assumed that there was no reason to keep the exchange secret, apart from the immoral nature of the bet in which it was involved.

"So you see, I really am sitting pretty," Stuart concluded. "The police are convinced now that the bloke who saw me outside Marksfield got the registration number wrong."

"Where did you leave the car when you got back?"

"In the lockup at the club, where I keep my own. It was still dark, and the lockup is fifty yards from the clubhouse itself. No one saw me or heard me. Don't fuss, old chap. Even if the constabulary did get suspicious again about the car, they'd still be stymied because there's absolutely nothing to connect me with you and your late lamented. That's the beauty of it. Or was, till you dragged me here to sick up your conscience into my lap."

A waft of wind blew, and a few yellowing leaves floated down from the tree above them.

"I don't like it," muttered Ned. Stuart Hammer stiffened, hearing a telltale quaver in his companion's voice. "I don't like it. Suppose the police start asking about my movements that Saturday night?"

"Why the hell should they? And if they were going to, they'd have done it already."

"That's what's getting me down. I feel they're just waiting their moment, waiting for me to crack up."

"Oh, bosh!"

Ned's head was bowed in his hands now, so that Stuart could hardly hear the muffled voice: "If they *did* ask me —I'm supposed to have been in Laura's flat the whole evening, but actually I didn't get there till long after midnight. Suppose they ask me what she and I were doing all the time—"

"That's an easy one," put in Stuart, with a short guffaw.

"Laura—I spun her a yarn—she'd back me up; but if they asked each of us separately to describe—well, what we had for supper, what we talked about, and so on—our statements wouldn't begin to tally."

"That's your funeral, old son."

"My funeral is yours too, don't forget."

"Well, you and Laura had better cook up the story together. How is the charming creature, by the way?"

"But—don't you see?—that'd make her suspicious of me. She'd start imagining the most awful things I must have been doing, and—"

"Oh, for God's sake, Ned, pull yourself together!" The bleeder's nearly in tears, thought Stuart: this has got to be stopped: he's simply not reliable. I ought to have seen he was the short-winded type when we were on the *Avocet*. The *Avocet* . . . A malignant expression darkened Stuart Hammer's face: his voice took on the man-to-man, sympathetic tone he adopted when discussing their grievances with his shop stewards.

"Tell me some more about this Brian Holmes. Decent fellow?"

Ned told him.

"Hard luck on the chap, certainly. Well, I suppose you can't let him be hanged."

"Or imprisoned for life."

"But it hasn't come to that yet. I think we should lie low a bit longer and wait to see how things pan out."

"And in the meantime the police may be catching up on us." The quavering note was back in Ned's voice.

"Well, exactly what's your proposition then?"

"That we should write a letter to Brian—a confession signed by both of us—setting out in detail what happened to Helena and your uncle. It would clear his mind of the fear he may be a murderer. But we'd appeal to him not to make any use of the document except in the event of his being put on trial and convicted."

Stuart Hammer inwardly whistled. He'd never heard such a fantastic proposal in his life. Ned must be round the bend. "You've got it all thought out, haven't you?" he commented quietly. "The answer is nix, old man. I'm not sticking my neck out that far."

"I'm sure Brian could be trusted."

"I admire your faith in human nature," said Stuart dryly. "No, no, it's not on the table."

"It seems to me you have no alternative."

"What the devil do you mean?"

"If you don't like my proposal, I told you I'd turn Queen's evidence. The former's a risk, but the latter's a certainty."

Bluff, a panicky twister's bluff, thought Stuart, scowling again at the obdurate back which Ned presented him. But *was* it bluff? Maybe the bastard really had gone off his rocker. Stuart Hammer took one of his rapid, ruthless decisions. "Well, you seem to have me by the short hairs," he said, putting a good-humored, rueful note into his voice. "Tell you what I'll do. If young Holmes is arrested, or if the police start turning the heat on you and me, we'll skip out of the country. The *Avocet* hasn't been laid up yet. I can put my hands on quite a packet of money at short notice, thanks to your bit of motoring at Norringham; and you'd better realize everything you can, too. We could nip over to Belgium before the dicks knew we were gone. I've contacts there who'd see us through to South America. We'd write our letter to Holmes on board, and post it from the continent. How's that strike you?"

"As a very sudden change of tune," replied Ned suspiciously.

"Well, you can take it or leave it. But don't imagine you'd get off scot free by turning Queen's evidence: you might save your neck, possibly, but you'd be jailed for a long, long stretch. Not nice."

Head in hands, Ned Stowe appeared to be ruminating. At last he said, "I suppose it is the best plan. Obviously, you and I sink or swim together now."

"I thought you'd come round, old son." Stuart Hammer inwardly exulted at the weakness he heard in Ned's voice: he'd mastered him, as before on the *Avocet,* by the strength of his own personality. "Now let's get everything straight, in case we do have to scarper."

They made plans for communicating with each other —a telephone call would have to be risked in certain emergencies. Stuart would pick up Ned at the same spot as on their previous voyage: it would preferably be at a weekend, so that Stuart could leave Norringham without advertising his departure. Ned must make sure his passport was in order, and collect all the money he could lay his hands on without rousing suspicion: it would not be much, for Helena's will had not yet been proved: however, Stuart would "see him through."

"And now I'll be toddling," said Stuart Hammer, after they had settled their arrangements. "See you later, if and when. Keep your pecker up, old boy." He rose, glancing at Ned's averted profile—a glance that had in it both contempt and calculation.

Ned watched him move away over the grass with his rolling gait, walk past a bed blazing with dahlias and chrysanthemums, and dwindle to a manikin size in the distance.

13   *The Bleeding Heart*

"WHAT HAVE you been doing all day, my darling?"

"Writing. My play. I'll have it finished tomorrow."

"Oh, that's wonderful!" said Laura. "We'll go out and celebrate tomorrow night, shall we? When can I read it?"

"When I—I've got to go away for the weekend. I'll leave the play to keep you company."

"Oh, I thought everything was cleared up at home— at the Old Farm. Funny, the way I still call it that. And I used to be so jealous of your life there."

"You didn't need to be."

Laura's broad white brow wrinkled as she bent over the socks she was knitting. "Do you feel this is your home now?"

"Well, we make a domestic enough scene, don't we, love?"

"Oh yes, I suppose so," she murmured vaguely; then, "Sometimes you seem more of a stranger than you used to in the old days."

189

"Mystery man, ha?"

There was a pause. A coal in the little fireplace spurted blue flame, hissing. Laura put down her work and looked full at Ned. "What's wrong, my love?"

"Wrong?"

"Your body's here with me. Your mind isn't."

"I'm tired, I expect." Ned began embroidering it. "When one's been concentrating on fictional characters —my play—it takes a bit of time to get back into focus with real ones."

"Yes." Laura pushed back one of her coppery tresses. "You do love me still?"

"I do love you still," he echoed, with a kind of gloomy fervor which made her search his face uneasily. What she found there did not altogether reassure her; but she was used to Ned's moods, and experience had taught her not to pry into men's minds when they had put the shutters up.

"Oh well," she said, without resentment or impatience.

It was the Thursday evening after Ned's meeting with Stuart Hammer. He had indeed spent the time writing his play, settling down to it every morning, going for a walk along the Embankment after lunch, and working again from 4 P.M. till Laura's return. By some mental freak, he was not only able to concentrate on his work, but the upheaval of his life since Helena had died, the turmoil of emotions in which he had been struggling, seemed to have thrown up to the surface a vein of talent far richer than any he had been able to tap before. He knew the play to be good. He had only to sharpen up the last scene a bit, and it would be finished. This afternoon, half an hour before Laura came home from work, Ned had found himself writing, on the back of the title page, *To Helena.* He had at once inked it out heavily; then, with an odd sensation of fear and release, he firmly inscribed the same dedication again.

Yes, the thing had gone incredibly smoothly, in a long gush of power which even Stuart Hammer's telephone call this morning had not checked.

"You-know-who speaking," the resonant, deep, hateful voice had announced. "I find I've got to take a cure. Doctor's orders. My health is *seriously* in danger. O.K. with you?"

"O.K."

After he had rung off, Ned speculated for a little about Hammer's situation. Had the police been questioning him again? or had the girl Peggy somehow been broken down? It was difficult to imagine a man of Stuart Hammer's type being panicked into throwing away the power and the money he had so ruthlessly schemed to secure. There was an alternative explanation for Hammer's recent action—an explanation Ned found it much easier to accept. His own course, at any rate, was decided: he had set the machine moving, and it was too late now to jump out of it, even if he wanted to. Ned recollected what Stuart had said to him on board the *Avocet,* when he had written the draft letter that should be sent to Laura in the event of his own failure to carry out his part of the compact. "Put in a bit at the end," Stuart had demanded, "saying that since her death, you've come to realize that you loved Helena better than anyone else." Ned remembered it now as one might remember a particu-

larly telling speech in a play seen weeks ago. It came
back to him with such force, he realized, because it
had come true. . . .

In the oddly shaped sitting room—it seemed to have
more corners than any small room had a right to—Laura
covertly eyed her lover, while the fire purred and snick-
ered in the grate. He looked calm, drained, withdrawn,
as though he had come through some major crisis in
which she had had no part, or made a decision from
which she was excluded. A little, vague flurry of apprehension stirred deep within her. It was as if, while he sat
there reading, Ned was slipping away from her and she
could do nothing to prevent it. At that moment Laura felt
an overmastering desire to have a child by him. Hugging
this desire like a secret, she said:

"I suppose we'll have to think of moving out of here
soon, Ned."

He came to himself with a start. "Moving out? Why?"

"Well, it's really much too small for the two of us."

"Yes. Yes, of course." Too small for the three of us,
he thought. And any house would be. Helena has settled
in, she will be wherever I am.

"And when there are three of us," Laura incredibly
echoed his thought.

"Three of us?" Ned stared at her.

"Yes, love. I want to have your child."

His heart surged with an overpowering emotion: then
at once came the backwash—the child of a confessed
murderer.

"Yes. But not yet, dear Laura," he said when he could
speak.

"You shall say when."

"I want it too. But"—he faltered and stopped, knowing it was both the truth and a lie.

"It's all right, my darling. I understand. You're not ready. And anyway," she added on a lighter note, "we're not married yet."

He looked at her gratefully. This divine acquiescence of hers, and this intuition of the times when he could not stand even the gentlest pressure, had from the start of their relationship moved him intensely. By contrast with Helena's exacting nature and the claustrophobic life he had lived with her, it made paradise—a paradise from which he must soon expel himself. For the first time since he had taken his decision, Ned faced squarely the consequence it would have for Laura. He knew she was not, as once she had seemed, invulnerable: that elusive quality, which had so tantalized and bewitched him, came not from self-sufficiency or coldness, he now saw, but was the effect of some deep feminine timidity, some fear of being too much involved—the very antithesis of her accepting passionate flesh: a sort of ingrained spiritual shyness.

Poor Laura. She would suffer. Why should there be the delusive notion that these women with big, easy bodies were somehow padded against the worst blows of anguish? He had betrayed Helena and his punishment was that he must betray Laura too. On paper, it should have been a simple choice between Laura's peace of mind and Brian Holmes's; but it was not a simple choice, for Helena all too ponderably entered into it.

Next morning Ned finished his play. When he had read it through for a last time, he typed out a fresh title page and wrote *For Laura with my love* upon the back of it. He must leave her with something, and to retain the dedication to Helena would be gratuitously cruel, self-indulgently sentimental. What good would Helena get out of it? Laura might at least feel it as some sort of substitute for the child they would never have.

In the afternoon, running sheets and carbon into his typewriter, he set to work upon the confession. It was a slow business, for he wanted it thorough: no detail must be omitted which might help the authorities, if the document came into their hands, to verify the fantastic course of events it described. The statement was objective, with no word of self-extenuation. When he had finished, he wrote a brief covering note to Brian Holmes's mother and put it with the carbon copy of the confession in a long envelope addressed to her.

It was now 4:20 P.M. Ned took a taxi to his club and ordered tea. While waiting for it, he asked an acquaintance to witness his signature.

"What's this, Stowe? A will, or a contract?" asked the man, as he bent to sign at the bottom of the folded sheet Ned placed before him.

"Neither. Or both," Ned replied.

"Oh well, I'll trust you."

"Many thanks."

Poor Stowe, the man thought; ghastly business about his wife—and the fellow who did it still at large. No wonder Stowe chokes people off nowadays: he must be feeling pretty raw still. Damned awkward, though, trying to offer condolences to a chap whose wife has been murdered. What the devil form of words *can* one use?

Ned drank his tea and left the club. On his way back to Chelsea he called in at an ironmonger's.

"Shall I wrap them up, sir?" asked the shopkeeper when he had made his purchase.

"What? Oh, no thanks. I'll put them in my pocket."

Queer type, thought the shopkeeper as Ned departed —looked as if he was sleepwalking.

When Ned returned to the flat, there were still two hours to go before he could expect Laura back. He laid and lit the fire: when it was burning well, he threw on it the pages of Helena's diary which he had been keeping in his wallet. There was no need for them any more: Helena was here, in possession of his mind, as though writing the confession had opened a door for her. He felt, not for the first time, a stranger in Laura's familiar little room. He and Helena were sitting here together, as it might be in a temporary resting place which they would never revisit, before putting on their coats again and going where they had to go.

Sitting by the fireside, Ned found himself reliving his past, which rose up before his mind's eye in a sequence of rapid, bright pictures, as it is said to do with a drowning man after he has ceased to struggle. The pictures were all of Helena—Helena and himself in the early days of their love or at those brief periods of reconciliation later which had deluded him with false hope. All these vividly recalled scenes had one thing in common: Helena was tender, or gay, or subdued, but never reproachful. And this, of itself, caused him the bitterest pang he had yet suffered. She had an unspeakable thing to reproach him with, *now,* but she did not do so. It was as if she had forgiven him for that; and what worse pains can a murderer be condemned to, he thought, than the forgiveness of his victim?

He struggled no more against the sea of self-reproach

that was engulfing him. Eager and golden, ruined and pathetic, Helena moved through his mind. Look on this picture, and on this. It was he who had wrought the dreadful change in her, he who had destroyed her, long before Stuart Hammer stopped her breath. More patience, more compassion and understanding on his part, and she would never have become what she did become: but again and again he had failed her, withdrawing into himself when he should have stretched out his hand to rescue her as she struggled. What he had justified as self-preservation, he saw now as cold, cowardly egotism. In the end, you do not preserve yourself by withdrawing your sympathy from a person for whom you are responsible, with whom you are so closely involved. Hardening his heart against her, he had atrophied it. He had created his own doom by failing to fight hard enough against hers.

Ned could feel again now. It felt as if the blood were running out of his heart, running to waste—a sensation so physically strong that he dragged himself from his chair and gazed into a mirror. A white, drained face looked out at him.

He began to pace about the little room, which had turned into a cage, desperately trying to wrench his mind away from Helena. Stuart Hammer's S.O.S., now—was it possible that the police really had got hold of something at Hammer's end of the conspiracy? But, if they had, surely they'd have questioned me by now about my movements on the night Herbert Beverley died? Perhaps they have interrogated Laura, though. She hasn't mentioned it to me; but she may be keeping quiet about it just to save me from worry.

Ned's overwrought mind could only respond dully to

this possibility of danger. What the police might have discovered was no longer important, unless it balked at the last moment the plan he had made for tomorrow. The plan involved, among other things, losing Laura; but this, Ned now realized, would not be the most painful part of his expiation. Not the most painful part for him. But for Laura?—how much would she suffer? Caught up inextricably in the coils of his own guilt, he could only expiate what he had done by giving mortal pain to a woman who loved him. In saving the innocent Brian Holmes, he would hurt the innocent Laura atrociously. It was an odd moment to be thinking of Laura's feelings, but Ned felt dimly glad that he was not too far gone to think of them.

When the bell rang, he caught his breath, convinced for a moment that it must be the police at last. But, opening the door, he saw Laura standing there alone.

"Lost your key?" he asked.

"No, love. I thought—I wanted you to come and open the door for me. It makes me feel as if I was really coming home."

This from the once cool, unsentimental Laura! The blood began to drain out of Ned's heart again.

While she dressed to go out with him, he summoned up all his little strength of mind to face the ordeal. If this was to be their last jaunt together, at least let him make it one which she would be happy to remember. He must act a part, he must create an illusion; to be dishonest now was, perhaps, the least dishonorable thing he could do.

As they walked into the restaurant, Laura created the usual impression. Ned was conscious of the way men looked at her and envied him. In the old days, when their meetings had to be secret, this had always made him uneasy: tonight it was merely ironic.

"You see?" he murmured. "They all want to take you home with them."

"Want must be their master," she demurely replied.

"Now you're going to eat the biggest dinner in your life. It's a celebration."

"You've really finished your play?"

"Yes. Down to the final curtain."

"Oh darling, how wonderful. And may I read it while you're away?"

"Of course. I've put it in your bureau. Complete with dedication."

"Dedication? To me, you mean?"

"Yes."

Swiftly she brushed her head against his shoulder. He saw there were tears in her eyes.

"You do know I love you," he said impulsively.

She nodded, unable to speak.

"Whatever happens, remember that."

"But nothing is going to happen? Is it?"

"No," he firmly replied.

Side by side on the plush seat against the wall, holding hands, they sipped their cocktails and ordered dinner. In the pinkish-gold light of the restaurant, Laura seemed to glow—cheek, neck, shoulder—like a classical goddess.

"It's wonderful being able to flaunt ourselves in public," she said, "instead of having to be furtive about it." Then, some time later, "You know, when you first came to me, I was frightened."

"Frightened?"

"That you'd never be able to get over Helena, after what had happened. You're such a broody old masochist."

"Masochist? I like that. You'll be telling me next it was

I, and not a dog at all, that took a bite out of my hand that night."

"Can you be arrested for biting yourself?"

"Only if it creates a public disturbance. Why?"

"I see why you asked me to give you an alibi, darling. You *had* bitten yourself in public, and it caused a riot. I'm not surprised."

"Lucky the police never questioned you about where I was that night," he said lightly. "You'd have caved in completely and landed me in the cooler for self-laceration."

"Oh no I wouldn't," she answered. "For you, I'd lie my soul away."

"Souls aren't got rid of so easily."

"Do you believe we have souls?" Laura was getting just the least bit tipsy. The way she said it made him feel, for the first time since they had come together, much older than she.

"Eat up your tournedos," he said, "and to hell with theology."

"I like you ordering me about," said Laura, pressing her thigh against his. "You'll go on doing it, won't you, when we're married?"

"Certainly I will. And bash you if you don't obey."

"I'd like that . . . Ned, what's the matter?" she asked sharply.

"Matter?"

"You suddenly looked—I don't know—implacable. Like a hanging judge. What is it?"

Ned's lighthearted remark had reminded him of what Stuart Hammer had done to Helena. "I was thinking of a man I'd like to kill," he said. "With my bare hands. What a ridiculous expression that is! As though it wouldn't be just as enjoyable if one wore gloves to do it."

"Ned! Don't talk like that!"

"Sorry."

"You mean, the man who—?"

"Yes."

Laura sighed involuntarily. Her beautiful shoulders drooped. Would Ned ever get away from Helena? She felt profoundly disheartened, realizing that all her efforts to give Ned peace of mind had been unavailing. It was unnatural, surely, for him still to be tied like this to a dead woman from whom he had struggled so hard to escape while she was alive. She wondered what Helena had been like—Ned had never been able to convey much about her—and what was the secret of her power over him: perhaps the secret was no more than that of a central weakness in Ned himself—a weakness which Laura was intuitively aware of, and toward which she felt a kind of affectionate impatience.

I must be a bit tight, she said to herself, crying over spilled milk like this. It's not Ned's fault. A thought stirred at the back of her mind. Ned's behavior ever since he had come to her that night, his alternations of sodden gloom and hectic passion or gaiety—it was that of a man trying to throw off remorse. Laura had assumed it was a sentimental remorse over the failure of his relationship with Helena. But there could be another explanation, whispered the voice at the back of her mind: isn't this just the way a murderer would behave? Remember what he said that first night?—"Would you still love me, supposing I told you I'd encouraged another man to kill her?"

No, it's quite fantastic, she angrily told herself, thrusting the thought away like a temptation. This is

Ned. I am sitting beside him. I love him. I know him through and through. He is a gentle, suffering man, not a monster.

All right, said the voice; but who is the man he'd like to kill with his bare hands? His accomplice? Himself?

"Let's have another bottle. I feel like getting tight this evening," said Laura.

"You shall. You're adorable when you're drunk. Like a loose-limbed doll."

Between them they did their best to rescue the evening from the blight which seemed to have fallen on it. They talked and laughed and made up indecent fantasies about their fellow diners. Laura was not quite steady on her feet when they left. She took Ned's hand, and held it inside the pocket of his mackintosh, their arms linked.

"What on earth have you got in your pocket, my darling?" she asked, as her hand came into contact with some objects there. "They feel like window wedges."

"They are window wedges, sweetheart."

"But our windows don't rattle."

"Oh, I thought they might come in useful," he vaguely replied.

14   *The Second Voyage*

STUART HAMMER rowed toward the derelict jetty, his oars taking deep gulps of water. There were not so many vessels in the outer anchorage of Yarwich harbor as when he had last picked up Ned Stowe here. The night was cold, and very dark. Behind the dinghy, the bare mast of *Avocet* at once disappeared from view: Hammer had not bent the sails: for this trip he would use the auxiliary, which was running very sweetly.

Everything was under control, provided Stowe turned up at the rendezvous. It *ought* to be all right. It was quite evident, when they were talking in Regent's Park, that the clot had lost his nerve: he had tried to bluster at first —all that stuff about turning Queen's evidence—but he had soon caved in. The only thing that worried Stuart Hammer was whether Stowe might have gone right round the bend since their meeting and said or done something irreparable. Anyone capable of supposing that he, Stuart Hammer, would tamely sign a joint confession and paddle off to South America must be soft in the head.

Well, the clot Stowe *was* soft, from truck to keel. He'd even bungled his little assignment in Norringham. Stuart Hammer did not really believe that Stowe would ever carry out his threats to write a confession which would put both their heads in nooses; but the risk was not worth taking: he could never feel safe with an unreliable type like Stowe knocking around. The bastard had fallen for his suggestion that they should skip out of the country, which showed how simple-minded he was. But that sort of simpleton could be dangerous.

So it was quite imperative that Ned Stowe should be disposed of. The method presented no complications to Hammer. He would put a strong sleeping draught in Ned's drink tonight, toss him into the middle of the North Sea, and chug quietly back to harbor.

The plan was as foolproof as their original one, and for the same reason—that there was no known connection between the two men. Stuart Hammer had impressed it on Ned, when they talked under the tree in Regent's Park, that he must not breathe a hint to anyone about where he was going today. If they were to get safely out of the country, Ned must cover his tracks from London to Yarwich. It pleased Stuart to think that Ned would be co-operating thus in his own doom.

He allowed the dinghy to drift the last twenty yards toward the jetty, which he identified at first not by sight, for it was still invisible in the blackness, but by the sound of waves splashing against it. Now he was near enough to descry a tall figure, motionless as a beacon, standing at the seaward end of the jetty.

Without a word spoken, Ned stepped into the dinghy, placed his bag in the stern sheets and took his place on the thwart beside Stuart Hammer. Together they rowed vigorously away from the land, whose dim outline was at once swept from view as though a hand had been placed over their eyes.

"Well, it's a good night for the job," muttered Ned, after they had rowed for a couple of minutes. "Always provided you can find your tub again in this darkness."

Stuart Hammer grunted, jerking a finger over one shoulder: "Riding light. You should be able to pick it up now."

Ned turned his head. A tiny light, which seemed to be hanging low down in the sky, was visible. "Good old *Avocet!*" he exclaimed.

"Pipe down! Sound travels over water."

They climbed on board and made the dinghy fast. It's just as it was the first night, thought Ned, feeling as if he had entered a recurrent nightmare: except that Hammer had a beard and an eyeshade then.

"Stow your baggage in the cabin. But don't turn on the light."

Ned pulled the solid teak door toward him and groped his way into the cabin. Taking an electric torch from his pocket, he flashed it cautiously around. Then he opened a locker, lifted out a pair of heavy sea boots and an oilskin. While he was putting them on, *Avocet* began to tremble, and Ned felt the thrust of the propeller as the engine was slipped into gear.

Back beside Hammer in the cockpit, the wind from the North Sea cold on his cheek, Ned said, "Well, here we are again. I suppose our journey really *is* necessary?"

"You suppose correctly, chum."

"Police twigged you?"

"I wouldn't say that. I'd not have been allowed to get this far if—"

"Well then, why are we scuttling off?"

"Because," said Stuart Hammer, improvising freely, "that bitch Peggy blew the gaff. Told the police on second thoughts she couldn't swear I'd been with her all that night. Told 'em she'd woken up next morning feeling as if she'd been drugged. They gave me a hell of a grilling after that. I stuck to my story: but I had a tip from the chief constable's office that they were beavering away again to trace the movements of the car I borrowed. It just wasn't good enough. I decided to get away while the going was good. So I rang you up. And here we are."

"It seems to me," commented Ned in a suspicious tone of voice, "you've been scared by your own shadow."

"It does, does it? Shall I put you ashore again, then?" Hammer snarled.

"Oh, I expect you're right."

"I damn well know I'm right. I've seen a bit of police work. Once they've got a thread in their hands, they don't let go. Sooner or later, they'd have hauled us in."

"I suppose so. But it's a hell of a prospect for me." Ned's voice began to tremble. "I shall never see Laura again."

The bloody wet, thought Hammer contemptuously—bleating about his popsy. And he has the infernal impudence to tell me I'm scared of my own shadow. I've a good mind to beat him up before I pitch him overboard. However, got to play him along for a bit—don't want him to get suspicious and swim for the shore.

"Well, it was your idea," he said. "Skip the country and then send the police a confession to clear young Holmes."

"That's true. It's just—oh well, we've got to sink or swim together."

Not together, son, not together, said Stuart Hammer to himself, grinning in the darkness. He peered ahead, feeling his way along the line of buoys which marked the channel. Ned glanced at his companion's hairy hand, firm on the tiller, and thought his own thoughts. Away on their port bow, the lighthouse at the headland scythed the water which led to open sea.

"Usual drill," said Stuart Hammer presently. "Go below while we pass the lighthouse."

Ned ducked into the cabin. Every ten seconds, as the beam struck through the portholes, the cabin sprang out of invisibility, then went black again, as if a flashlight photograph were being taken of him. All this had happened before, in another life. Ned's mind felt clear and cold. Would Laura be asleep by now, or lying in the darkness thinking about last night, planning their future together? He saw her suddenly, standing at the street door this morning, in her characteristic attitude of good-by—quite motionless, one hand tentatively raised, her eyes gazing fixedly upon him. She had always said good-by thus, with that fixed, deeply inquiring look, as though she wondered if it was not good-by forever. Well, this time it was.

He heard the tread of heavy boots overhead, going forward, then returning. When Stuart Hammer called him out a few minutes later, Ned observed that the navigation lights had been extinguished.

"Just in case the balloon has gone up and they're searching for us," said Hammer.

"Suits me."

"You weren't trailed to Yarwich by any types in mackintoshes and large boots, I suppose?" asked Stuart affably.

"Not so as you'd notice. I told Laura I had to go back to Crump End for a couple of days, to settle things up. I drove thirty miles out of London, put my car in a garage, pottered about the countryside for most of the day, then took a bus back to town and caught the last train down to Yarwich. If anyone had been shadowing me, I'd have spotted him during my country walk."

"Sounds O.K. to me. What it is to have a brain!"

"The trouble is, I've got damned little dough with me. I drew out what I had in my own account, but I can't touch Helena's capital yet."

"Don't worry about that, old man. I'll see you through all right."

"Where do you plan to make for? Isn't the Continent rather risky? They might be on the lookout for us at the ports."

"Take it easy, old man. It's all lined up. Trust your Uncle Stu."

The *Avocet* was sidling and swerving through an awkward cross-sea. Without the sails to steady her, she bucked at times in a disquieting, eccentric way, though the waves were nothing formidable. To be seasick now would be a monstrous irrelevance, thought Ned sourly.

"May I drive her for a bit?" he asked. "It'd take my mind off my stomach."

"Presently. It's an awkward patch here in an offshore wind. She'll settle down before long, you'll find."

For a while Ned watched the waves rearing and tumbling behind *Avocet*'s quarter, baring their teeth now and then in a snarl of foam.

"By the way," he said, "I've written the document."

"What document?"

"The confession."

Stuart Hammer's knuckles went white on the tiller. "You've written it? Already? What the hell's the idea of that?"

"To put Brian Holmes out of his misery, of course. We agreed that—"

"We agreed to do it together, *after* we'd got away," Stuart interrupted with ominous calm. Then his self-control broke. "My God, you unspeakably silly little clot, I could break your neck! Do you realize what you've done? Do you suppose Holmes'll keep it to himself? You must be insane! Every police force in Europe'll be alerted. When did you post the damned thing?"

"Well, what an exhibition of hysteria!" remarked Ned coldly. "I never said I'd *posted* it."

"You never—" Stuart gasped for breath then let loose a flood of foul language. There was foam at the corners of his mouth. "I shouldn't advise you to play games with me," he ended, menacingly, when he had calmed down a bit. "Where is the thing?"

"In my breast pocket."

"Hand it over, son."

"Why the hell should I?"

"I said, hand it over."

Ned Stowe shrugged his shoulders. "Oh well," he said, "if you insist," and passed a folded sheaf of papers to his companion. Keeping a wary eye on him, Stuart Hammer studied the top sheet by the dim light of the binnacle. "This seems to be all in order, but it's staying in my possession from now on. And in future kindly follow *my* instructions. Carrying a thing like this about! Suppose you'd lost it, or been pickpocketed."

"I never thought of that," said Stowe in a dismal tone.

"So it seems." Stuart Hammer grinned evilly. "In fact, you're a bloody wet, eh?"

The other man was silent.

"Well?" said Hammer.

"Well what?"

"I asked you a question. I like people to answer when I ask them questions."

"Don't be ridiculous."

Stuart Hammer's hand shot out, and his fingers dug into Ned's biceps; the pain was excruciating.

"Well?" said Hammer again.

"I've forgotten what you asked me. For Christ's sake!"

"I said 'you're a bloody wet, aren't you?'"

"Oh, all right, all right." Ned Stowe sounded as if he was almost weeping.

"That's no answer," Hammer gently remarked.

"All right then, I'm a bloody wet."

"That's better." Hammer took his hand away. It gave him intense satisfaction to have humiliated Ned Stowe. There only remained now to kill him. He would have enjoyed doing it slowly, with Ned conscious—he owed him something for that crack about an "exhibition of hysteria"; but a life-and-death struggle on a small ship was attended by too much risk, even with a weakling like Stowe: a cant of the deck might send them both overboard.

"Look after her for a bit, will you," he said curtly. "I'm going to run us up some coffee. Throttle here. Keep her as she's going."

"Very well," Ned sullenly replied, not meeting his companion's eye. Stuart Hammer entered the cabin, drew the curtains across the portholes and switched on a low-powered light over the stove. While he waited for the water to boil, he shook a white powder out into one of the two mugs.

Ned Stowe, holding the tiller loosely, strained his eyes into the darkness ahead. They should be crossing the coastal traffic lane quite soon. Rapidly he lashed the helm, then took from his pocket four window wedges, moved in a few strides along the cockpit, and with his heavy boots kicked the wedges firmly into position under the edge of the cabin door.

"What do you want now?" called Stuart Hammer, thinking he had heard Ned knock on the door.

"Nothing. I was just wondering if you were lonely in there."

"Get back to the helm."

"Because you *will* be."

"What's that?"

"Nothing."

Ned turned to the helm. His eyes were accustomed to the dark now, and he could see tiny lights, pinpricks in the night, ahead on the port and starboard bows. He opened the throttle to full speed. The sooner he got into the coastal traffic lane, the better: the wedges should hold all right, but if Stuart Hammer had an axe or a marlin-spike in there, he might, given time, batter through the door, solid teak though it was.

In fact, he was battering now, with his fists.

Ned slid closer to the door. "What's the matter now?" he shouted.

"The bloody door seems to have jammed. And who the hell told you to put on speed?"

"I like going fast. What did you say about the door?"

"It's jammed. Can't understand it. Never happened before."

"Well, of course it's jammed. Didn't you hear me kicking the wedges underneath it?"

There was a full thirty seconds of silence from within. The thump and brush of the waves, like a jazz drummer's continuo, swelled louder. Ned imagined Stuart Hammer on his knees, trying to look under the door and locate the wedges, poking at them ineffectually with a penknife. But the door fitted snugly: Hammer hadn't a hope.

"I'll murder you for this when I get out," he suddenly bellowed, thumping again on the door.

"That's why you're not getting out," called Ned. "But you were going to murder me anyway, weren't you?"

"I don't know what you mean."

Ned edged closer to the door, so that he did not have to shout. He spoke loud and clear:

"The trouble with you, little man, is that you're all conceit and no brains. You consistently overrate yourself, and therefore underrate everyone else. In fact—can you hear me?—you're just a vulgar little red-faced nonentity."

The man within bawled abuse.

"Do you really suppose," Ned continued, "that I was taken in by your ridiculous maneuvers when we met last? A child would have seen through them. I pretended to collapse, to agree that we should leave the country together. It suited my book, you see—it was exactly what I was leading you on to suggest. All this stuff about the police being after you is pure invention on your part. You were determined to get rid of me because you thought I was cracking up. I deliberately gave you that impression, and you fell for it like the sucker you are. The last thing you ever intended to do was to sign the confession. Well, one signature on it will be enough to reassure Brian Holmes.''

"You must be mad," came Stuart Hammer's voice. "I have the confession here."

"I was mad last time I sailed with you. I've been getting saner ever since. You've got *one* copy of the confession. I posted another—with my signature on it witnessed—to Brian Holmes a few hours ago, from Yarwich. Oh yes, and I told him in a covering letter what my plans are for you and me."

There was a short silence. Then Stuart Hammer spoke, in a humoring tone very different from his previous bluster. Ned smiled, detecting that Hammer's confidence had at last begun to fray.

"Your plans, old man? I simply don't get it. What's in your mind?"

"Hatred," Ned calmly answered. "You're going to pay for what you did to Helena."

"But, damn it, you agreed, you wanted—"

"Oh, I'm going to pay too, don't you worry."

Breaking off, Ned moved back to the stern and gazed ahead. The lights of the coastal shipping were closer now —a mile away, perhaps, though he had no skill at judging sea distances in the dark. Overhead, the tall mast rocked gently as *Avocet* sidled over the swell. Stuart Hammer was beating on the cabin door again. Ned jumped down into the cockpit. He felt an extraordinary sense of physical well-being.

"Getting lonely?" he shouted to the other.

"Look here, old man, a joke's a joke. You've had your fun. Let's call it off. I'm sorry if I was a bit tough with you just now."

"You'll be sorrier that you were a bit tough with Helena."

Ned Stowe peered forward again. With the helm lashed, *Avocet* was keeping her course well enough. He moved closer to the cabin door.

"I was going to tell you about my plans," he began in conversational tones. "Remember last time we sailed together? You tested my nerve, shaving that cargo liner. Well, tonight I'm going to test yours. In about twenty minutes we shall cross the coastal shipping lane. It was very helpful of you, by the way, to put out the navigation lights. The *Avocet* is quite invisible. The cabin portholes are too near the water for your light in there to be seen by a lookout on a ship's bridge—until it's too late, anyway."

"What the devil do you mean, 'too late'?"

"I propose to run across the bows of the largest vessel available out there. I'm not very expert at it, so I may miss the first one; but there'll be plenty more, and it'd give you more time to contemplate your end. Something was said about sinking or swimming together. I doubt if you'll get any chance to swim, little man."

"My God! You *are* crazy. You'll never get away with it."

"But I don't want to get away with it."

There was an appalled silence from within, then another fusillade of blows on the cabin door. When Hammer finally left off, Ned remarked:

"Losing your nerve already? You're going to be in a dreadful state by the time we have our collision. Well, I must be leaving you for a while. Why not settle down and read a good book?"

"Here, stop! Wait a minute! Ned, I'll give you money, anything you ask. I'll write you a check—yes, pass it under the door—you needn't let me out till—"

"How much money?"

"Five thousand. Ten," Hammer wildly shouted. "Wait! I'm just writing it now."

A slip of paper appeared under the door. Ned took it to the binnacle light. A check for £10,000, duly if shakily signed. He held it up between two fingers for a moment, then allowed the wind to snatch it away.

"Too bad," he said, near the door again. "The wind blew it overboard."

"I'll write another."

"Oh, shut up! Keep your breath to drown with. You'll suffocate in there when we collide. Quite slowly, I hope. Like you suffocated Helena. You're caught, and you can't get out. But the worst part won't be the drowning, I daresay: it'll be the waiting for the impact. It'll seem like hours. Sweat it out, little man, sweat it out."

Ned returned to the helm and unlashed it. However enjoyable the thought of Stuart Hammer's state of mind, for himself he wanted to get it over. He was near enough now to the coastal traffic to see the ships' lights moving against the black backcloth. He picked out one set of lights, a good distance away to northward, as the executioner.

There was a new sound from inside the cabin—a measured thudding which suggested that Stuart Hammer had got to work with a marlinspike or an ax; if the latter, he would be able to break through the door before long. Ned groped in a locker beneath him and found a marlinspike. He did not want to kill Hammer that way, but it might be necessary.

The thudding went on for some time, then stopped. It was evidently not an ax. Ned moved forward a moment, to make sure the wedges had not shifted. Now he could steer his course undistracted. The vessel he had picked on was coming up fast, but he judged it would pass astern of him if he maintained his present speed, for already he could see both its starboard and port navigation lights. He throttled back, letting *Avocet* idle over the waves.

He became aware that the waves were lighting up and darkening in a curious way. For a moment he thought something had gone wrong with his eyes. Then he realized that the light came from *Avocet's* cabin portholes just above deck level: Stuart Hammer had opened the curtains and was switching the lights on and off to attract attention—switching them, Ned quickly perceived, to make the Morse signal of S.O.S.

Ned's brain was working with remarkable clarity and resource. He put down the helm, so that *Avocet* came round to port and was soon pointing almost dead straight at the approaching vessel, instead of showing her broadside. Now a lookout on the vessel would not be able to see the *Avocet's* lighted portholes.

Stuart Hammer's next move took him by surprise. He had been watching over the port bow the lights of the approaching steamer, toward which he was steering, now that the course was altered, at a fine angle. Something caught his eye—a movement rather than an object— between the *Avocet's* deck and the night. He flashed his torch on it. A cylindrical shape was protruding from one of the portholes, pointing outward and skyward. Snatching up the marlinspike, Ned clambered onto the half-deck, ran forward, and struck viciously downward at the distress rocket which Stuart Hammer had pushed through the open porthole and was about to fire off. The rocket fell on the deck and Ned kicked it into the sea. If Hammer had succeeded in releasing it, every vessel in sight would have been on the alert.

It was annoying that Hammer should distract him while he wanted to concentrate upon his steering. *Avocet's* head had fallen off during this brief skirmish, and she would be showing her broadside again, with its four lighted portholes, to the advancing steamer. Jumping to the helm, Ned swung her back onto course. Would Hammer try that one again? Had he a supply of rockets in the cabin? Ned warily watched, shifting his gaze between the port and starboard sides of the cabin and the navigating lights of the steamer which was racing toward them.

What had annoyed him most, he now realized, was that Stuart Hammer should have recovered his nerve—to the extent, anyway, of showing some resourcefulness. He had wanted to reduce the man to a state of bellowing, blubbering panic before he killed him. But this cold vindictiveness now left him. He had no desire to bait Stuart Hammer any more. It was no longer a question of avenging Helena's death—only of expiating it. He was as guilty as Stuart and the world would be well rid of them both. The quicker the better.

The advancing steamer grew out of the darkness ahead, a dim bulk rapidly enlarging itself. Opening the throttle full, Ned drove *Avocet* to intercept the flutter of foam at the vessel's stem. Far too late, Stuart Hammer let off another rocket from a starboard porthole. Its only effect, when it burst high overhead, was to draw the eyes of the lookouts upward for the few remaining seconds during which *Avocet* would have been visible to them.

Then, screened from their view by the steamer's ponderous, high fo'c'sle, *Avocet* swung sharply to starboard as Ned put the helm up and ran her at right angles across the steamer's course. Peering through a porthole, Stuart Hammer saw the great bows ripping toward him like a vertical knife, an advancing promontory, and had time only to shriek once before the impact hurled him off his feet and the inrushing sea began to strangle him.

The vessel had struck *Avocet* dead amidships. The stem rolled her over, trod her down, thrust her aside, leaving a shattered and waterlogged hulk sinking in the steamer's wake. Ned Stowe was flung into the sea by the impact. He rose once to the surface, then the heavy sea boots dragged him down for good.

THE PERENNIAL LIBRARY MYSTERY SERIES

E. C. Bentley

TRENT'S LAST CASE
"One of the three best detective stories ever written." —Agatha Christie

TRENT'S OWN CASE
"I won't waste time saying that the plot is sound and the detection satisfying.
Trent has not altered a scrap and reappears with all his old humor and
charm." —Dorothy L. Sayers

Gavin Black

A DRAGON FOR CHRISTMAS
"Potent excitement!" —New York Herald Tribune

THE EYES AROUND ME
"I stayed up until all hours last night reading *The Eyes Around Me*, which is
something I do not do very often, but I was so intrigued by the ingeniousness
of Mr. Black's plotting and the witty way in which he spins his mystery. I can
only say that I enjoyed the book enormously." —F. van Wyck Mason

YOU WANT TO DIE, JOHNNY?
"Gavin Black doesn't just develop a pressure plot in suspense, he adds
uninfected wit, character, charm, and sharp knowledge of the Far East to
make rereading as keen as the first race-through." —Book Week

Nicholas Blake

THE BEAST MUST DIE
"It remains one more proof that in the hands of a really first-class writer the
detective novel can safely challenge comparison with any other variety of
fiction." —The Manchester Guardian

THE CORPSE IN THE SNOWMAN
"If there is a distinction between the novel and the detective story (which we
do not admit), then this book deserves a high place in both categories."
—The New York Times

THE DREADFUL HOLLOW
"Pace unhurried, characters excellent, reasoning solid."
—San Francisco Chronicle

END OF CHAPTER
" ...admirably solid...an adroit formal detective puzzle backed up by firm
characterization and a knowing picture of London publishing."
—The New York Times

HEAD OF A TRAVELER
"Another grade A detective story of the right old jigsaw persuasion."
—*New York Herald Tribune Book Review*

MINUTE FOR MURDER
"An outstanding mystery novel. Mr. Blake's writing is a delight in itself."
—*The New York Times*

THE MORNING AFTER DEATH
"One of Blake's best." —Rex Warner

A PENKNIFE IN MY HEART
"Style brilliant ... and suspenseful." —*San Francisco Chronicle*

A QUESTION OF PROOF
"The characters in this story are unusually well drawn, and the suspense is
well sustained." —*The New York Times*

THE SAD VARIETY
"It is a stunner. I read it instead of eating, instead of sleeping."
—Dorothy Salisbury Davis

THE SMILER WITH THE KNIFE
"An extraordinarily well written and entertaining thriller."
—*Saturday Review of Literature*

THOU SHELL OF DEATH
"It has all the virtues of culture, intelligence and sensibility that the most
exacting connoisseur could ask of detective fiction."
—*The Times* [London] *Literary Supplement*

THE WHISPER IN THE GLOOM
"One of the most entertaining suspense-pursuit novels in many seasons."
—*The New York Times*

THE WIDOW'S CRUISE
"A stirring suspense....The thrilling tale leaves nothing to be desired."
—*Springfield Republican*

THE WORM OF DEATH
"It [The Worm of Death] is one of Blake's very best—and his best is better
than almost anyone's." —Louis Untermeyer

Edmund Crispin

BURIED FOR PLEASURE
"Absolute and unalloyed delight." —Anthony Boucher, *The New York Times*

Kenneth Fearing

THE BIG CLOCK
"It will be some time before chill-hungry clients meet again so rare a compound of irony, satire, and icy-fingered narrative. *The Big Clock* is...a psychothriller you won't put down."   —*Weekly Book Review*

Andrew Garve

A HERO FOR LEANDA
"One can trust Mr. Garve to put a fresh twist to any situation, and the ending is really a lovely surprise."   —*The Manchester Guardian*

THE ASHES OF LODA
"Garve ... embellishes a fine fast adventure story with a more credible picture of the U.S.S.R. than is offered in most thrillers."
        —*The New York Times Book Review*

THE CUCKOO LINE AFFAIR
" ... an agreeable and ingenious piece of work."   —*The New Yorker*

THE FAR SANDS
"An impeccably devious thriller....The quality is well up to Mr. Garve's high standard of entertainment."   —*The New Yorker*

MURDER THROUGH THE LOOKING GLASS
"...refreshingly out-of-the-way and enjoyable...highly recommended to all comers."   —*Saturday Review*

NO TEARS FOR HILDA
"It starts fine and finishes finer. I got behind on breathing watching Max get not only his man but his woman, too."   —Rex Stout

THE RIDDLE OF SAMSON
"The story is an excellent one, the people are quite likable, and the writing is superior."   —*Springfield Republican*

Michael Gilbert

BLOOD AND JUDGMENT
"Gilbert readers need scarcely be told that the characters all come alive at first sight, and that his surpassing talent for narration enhances any plot.... Don't miss."   —*San Francisco Chronicle*

THE BODY OF A GIRL
"Does what a good mystery should do: open up into all kinds of ramifications, with untold menace behind the action. At the end, there is a bang-up climax, and it is a pleasure to see how skilfully Gilbert wraps everything up."   —*The New York Times Book Review*

THE DANGER WITHIN

"Michael Gilbert has nicely combined some elements of the straight detective story with plenty of action, suspense, and adventure, to produce a superior thriller." —*Saturday Review*

DEATH HAS DEEP ROOTS

"Trial scenes superb; prowl along Loire vivid chase stuff; funny in. right places; a fine performance throughout." —*Saturday Review*

FEAR TO TREAD

"Merits serious consideration as a work of art." —*The New York Times*

C. W. Grafton

BEYOND A REASONABLE DOUBT

"A very ingenious tale of murder ... a brilliant and gripping narrative."
—Jacques Barzun and Wendell Hertig Taylor

Cyril Hare

AN ENGLISH MURDER

"By a long shot, the best crime story I have read for a long time. Everything is traditional, but originality does not suffer. The setting is perfect. Full marks to Mr. Hare." —*Irish Press*

UNTIMELY DEATH

"The English detective story at its quiet best, meticulously underplayed, rich in perceivings of the droll human animal and ready at the last with a neat surprise which has been there all the while had we but wits to see it."
—*New York Herald Tribune Book Review*

WHEN THE WIND BLOWS

"The best, unquestionably, of all the Hare stories, and a masterpiece by any standards." —Jacques Barzun and Wendell Hertig Taylor, *A Catalogue of Crime*

WITH A BARE BODKIN

"One of the best detective stories published for a long time."
—*The Spectator*

James Hilton

WAS IT MURDER?

"The story is well planned and well written." —*The New York Times*

Francis Iles

BEFORE THE FACT
"Not many 'serious' novelists have produced character studies to compare with Iles's internally terrifying portrait of the murderer in *Before the Fact*, his masterpiece and a work truly deserving the appellation of unique and beyond price."
—Howard Haycraft

MALICE AFORETHOUGHT
"It is a long time since I have read anything so good as *Malice Aforethought*, with its cynical humour, acute criminology, plausible detail and rapid movement. It makes you hug yourself with pleasure."
—H. C. Harwood, *Saturday Review*

Lange Lewis

THE BIRTHDAY MURDER
"Almost perfect in its playlike purity and delightful prose."
—Jacques Barzun and Wendell Hertig Taylor

Arthur Maling

LUCKY DEVIL
"The plot unravels at a fast clip, the writing is breezy and Maling's approach is as fresh as today's stockmarket quotes." —*Louisville Courier Journal*

RIPOFF
"A swiftly paced story of today's big business is larded with intrigue as a Ralph Nader-type investigates an insurance scandal and is soon on the run from a hired gun and his brother....Engrossing and credible." —*Booklist*

SCHROEDER'S GAME
"As the title indicates, this Schroeder is up to something, and the unravelling of his game is a diverting and sufficiently blood-soaked entertainment."
—*The New Yorker*

Julian Symons

THE BELTING INHERITANCE
"A superb whodunit in the best tradition of the detective story."
—August Derleth, *Madison Capital Times*

BLAND BEGINNING
"Mr. Symons displays a deft storytelling skill, a quiet and literate wit, a nice feeling for character, and detectival ingenuity of a high order."
—Anthony Boucher, *The New York Times*

THE COLOR OF MURDER
"A singularly unostentatious and memorably brilliant detective story."
—*New York Herald Tribune Book Review*

THE 31ST OF FEBRUARY
"Nobody has painted a more gruesome picture of the advertising business since Dorothy Sayers wrote 'Murder Must Advertise', and very few people have written a more entertaining or dramatic mystery story."
—*The New Yorker*